Shared

The Pleasure Collection, Volume 2

Jasmine Black

Published by Spunky Girl Publishing, 2023.

Shared

Jasmine Black

Jasmine Black brings you "Shared" ~ Book Two in her Pleasure Collection series. In this book you'll find eight ménage erotica short stories including taken by doctors, bikers, billionaires, bosses, cowboys, firefighters, personal trainers and carpenters!

Don't forget to also grab Pleasured by Her Guards ~ Book One in Jasmine Black's Pleasure Collection series where you'll find three ménage erotica short stories with naughty male guards who take the women they want!

Taken by Two Doctors
Jasmine Black
Waitress Jean Spelling visits her controversial doctor once a month for some much-needed...stress relief. She looks forward to putting her feet up in the stirrups and enjoys Dr. Ball's naughty unconventional treatments. This time when she arrives, she's surprised to discover that she'll be physically examined by two doctors and they'll prescribe her some much-needed stress release right there on the examination table!

~~

Taken by Two Bikers
Jasmine Black

~

When waitress Zoe Miller's car breaks down late one night on a deserted road, she's thankful her biker ex-boyfriend and his best friend come to her rescue...in more ways than one!

~

Taken by Two Bosses
Jasmine Black
Trapped in the company elevator, receptionist Carina Chantilli is suddenly at the mercy of her two sexy bosses...
Taken By Two Billionaires
Jasmine Black

~

Jill has always been warned that her gambling lifestyle would get her into trouble. And now *she's in trouble.*

She's lost a poker game to two very sexy billionaires and they want *her* as their winnings.

They'll to do her whatever they wish...for an entire year.

On her way to her new life in Italy, while in a white stretch limo, Franco and Gianni will show Jill exactly what it means *to be won* by two billionaires.

~~

Taken by Two Cowboys
Jasmine Black

~~

Sierra Allan works hard at her late-father's horse ranch. When her step-brother adds her handy girl services to a private auction to help raise money for the failing ranch, she figures there's no harm...but she's stunned when she's "sold" to two sexy cowboys who demand she submit to their dark desires...

~

Taken by Two Firefighters
Jasmine Black

Firefighter Kendall Farell has always been attracted to the erotic beauty of the hot flames that dance in burning buildings. Her dangerous fetish could cost her her job if anyone ever finds out. When she's caught flirting with fire and rescued from certain death, her two male co-workers want payback in a very naughty way...

~

Taken by Two Personal Trainers
Jasmine Black

~

When dancer Chelsea White discovers her lucrative job is in jeopardy, she hires an extreme team to whip her back into physical shape. But her two personal trainers aren't going to give her just any regular gym exercises...

~

Taken by Two Carpenters
Jasmine Black

~

A gift certificate from her three besties has Colleen Rue ordering an extravagant pleasure machine from The Sexy Wooden Toy Shoppe, but she quickly discovers that the two well-muscled carpenters have much more in mind than just showing her how the machine works...

Shared

Published by Spunky Girl Publishing
Print Copyright 2023 Jasmine Black
Cover Art by Talina Perkins ~ Bookin' It Designs

License Notes
This book is licensed for your personal use only.

~

Author Note
This is a work of fiction. Characters, places, settings, and events presented in this book are purely of the author's imagination and bear no resemblance to any actual person, living or dead or to any actual events, places, and/or settings.

Taken by Two Doctors

Jasmine Black

Waitress Jean Spelling visits her controversial doctor once a month for some much-needed...stress relief. She looks forward to putting her feet up in the stirrups and enjoys Dr. Ball's naughty unconventional treatments. This time when she arrives, she's surprised to discover that she'll be physically examined by two doctors and they'll prescribe her some much-needed stress release right there on the examination table!

Chapter One

Sky-blue eyes riveted to my face as I entered the doctor's examination room.

Inside the room was a lean man, around my age of twenty-five. I'd never seen him before, yet he wore the traditional white doctor's coat, and sat at the doctor's desk writing something on some paper, acting as if he belonged there.

His hair was brown and somewhat long for a medical professional. He even had a sexy dark five o'clock shadow on his chin and cheeks that I found quite attractive.

I assumed he was the new doctor-in-training who would be helping Dr. Ball with his incredibly busy and controversial practice involving stress relief.

"Have a seat, Jean." His voice was clear, crisp, and business-like, but when I sat down on the chair beside his desk, I trembled at the sizzling way his gaze wandered over the swell of my breasts that pushed up against my silky summer blouse.

It had been hot working all day in the local diner, and it was even hotter in the doctor's waiting room. I was the last appointment of the day and no one had been around while I'd waited, so I'd unbuttoned the two top blouse buttons, allowing some air to get to the perspiring valley of my breasts. In the way he was gawking, he was getting a nice view of my assets.

"I'm Dr. Smith. I believe you're here for your monthly stress release physical, right?" he asked.

The intense way he was staring at me made me think that, yes, this doctor was going to do some wickedly delicious things to me just like the other one did. Did he know about my medical fetish? Did he know how aroused I got being around anything to do with doctors in white lab coats?

"Yes." I sounded too breathy. I was too eager for this physical to start. My regular doctor did some naughty things to me...down there, when he did an exam.

I know it isn't traditional to have monthly physicals, but I like how my doctor touches me. I like how my breasts swell as he pinches my nipples with his forceps. I really enjoy how my pussy creams and how I tremble every time he rubs my clit with one of his naughty medical instruments. I always know that by the way his breaths get faster and faster that he is excited to be touching me.

It has become a monthly routine. He'd end our session by "saying see you next month," and I would nod. With my every visit to his office, he gets bolder with me. I like it.

Last time, he'd touched me so perfectly, I'd been so close to begging him to take me that when he'd finished with my internal exam, I had been barely able to get my feet out of the stirrups. My legs had been so weak and my pussy so wet, I had masturbated right out in my car in the doctor's parking lot. I'm pretty sure he'd been watching from his office window because I'd seen his blinds move. And I noticed, too, how his incredibly huge bulge had pressed against his pants every time he'd left the exam room.

"Well, let's get down to work then. Remove all your clothing and hop onto the examination table," the new doctor said. His voice snapped me back to reality.

I waited for him to give me one of those flimsy paper gowns like Dr. Ball did, and for him to leave so I could undress.

He didn't leave. He just went back to writing on a pad on the desk.

Oh. This was an interesting twist.

After a moment, he noticed I hadn't moved and his head turned to look at me. There was a trace of a dark lust glittering in his blue eyes and I noticed how his gaze settled upon my lips.

Wicked anticipation snapped through me.

"Is there a problem?" he asked. I liked the heavy-lidded, sensual look of his eyes. His smell was clean and fresh, just like the office and the medical instruments.

"Um, aren't you supposed to leave?" I asked.

His dark brows lifted and he chuckled lightly. "I can't examine you if I leave."

He had a point. What difference would a few minutes make? He'd eventually see me naked anyway.

His heated blue gaze watched me with great interest as I began undressing. A moment of shyness caught me and I turned away to unbutton my blouse. After my blouse and pants were removed, I jumped with surprise as his sizzling hands curled around my waist. This doctor might be a bit bolder than the other one.

"Are you nervous?" he asked as he pressed himself against my back. His erection pushed against my panty-clad butt and I inhaled as the carnal shivers of excitement rippled through me.

"Isn't what you're doing against the law?" I asked him.

I whimpered as his hot lips touched my earlobe.

"I get a rush doing things the illegal way. Don't you?"

Chapter Two

Damn. So Dr. Ball must have told him about how often she came here and how he found all kinds of excuses to bill my insurance company for my frequent naughty visits.

I closed my eyes as I inhaled a shuddering breath. Why did I get the feeling this doctor was going to bring my physical to an entirely new level?

"Are you sexually active?" he asked. He sounded gruff.

It was a normal question Dr. Ball would ask me, but in the way this guy asked — in a low, sexy voice — that gave me the impression he was personally curious.

"It's been a while. I have a problem with orgasms," I admitted.

"Ahh, yes. Dr. Ball explained you need medical interventions for your release. Here, let me help you with your bra and panties."

Oh dear. Definitely a bolder doctor.

I held my breath as his long hot fingers slipped inside the elastic band of my panties. He slid them over my buttocks and down my legs and off. Then his hot fingers unclasped my bra, and he seductively and slowly pushed the straps over my shoulders. It fell away and my perky breasts bounced free. He turned me to face him.

My pussy creamed with wet heat as his scorching gaze fixed on my two mounds. I noticed a muscle twitch in his jaw. He ripped his gaze from my breasts and patted the examination bed.

"Okay, hop up on the table. Dr. Ball will join us in a minute."

I swallowed nervously. "Join us?"

"Yes, he's asked me to assist him, with your problem."

Oh. Wow.

Something electrical ignited deep inside my pussy. *Two doctors touching me?* Suddenly, I could barely breathe at the erotic thought.

Dr. Ball moved away from me, but he kept his eyes glued to my bouncy breasts as I climbed on the table and sat down.

11

"Lie down," he instructed.

I swung my legs up and lay down on the comfortable padded table. A moment later, he moved closer and his heated fingers clasped my left ankle and raised it high into the stirrup. Then he lifted my other leg into the other stirrup. I inhaled at the feel of first one leather ankle restraint being placed and then the other also being strapped.

Then Dr. Ball proceeded to lash my wrists at my sides with leather restraints that he'd brought up from beneath the examination bed.

I lay very naked, my wrists and ankles secured, my knees bent and close up to my chest, and my thighs spread widely apart. I creamed warmly as I stared up at the ceiling, loving this position of helplessness.

I trembled as the doctor walked to the foot of the bed. He stared between my widespread legs, his scorching gaze caressing my cunt. I creamed some more.

I could feel the hot gush sliding down my vagina as I secretly hoped he would climb up on the bed, lay on top of me, and start hammering his cock into me. I swear I would have asked him to do just that when the door flew open and my regular doctor walked into the room.

Immediately, I relaxed. Well, just a little. It was nice to see his familiar face. I'd always found him cute. He was a bit older than me and he wore his hair combed back off his face. He had sweet brown eyes and he always had a welcoming smile for me. He was doing just that as he glanced over at me.

"Hello. Long time no see, Jean. Are you ready for your stress release?"

I nodded.

To my surprise, my face heated as both doctors stood side by side at the foot of the bed and did a visual inspection, their gazes roaming along my breasts, over my belly and ending between my thighs.

"I'll get the instruments," Dr. Smith said. He grabbed a towel-covered tray off the desk and placed it on a nearby rollaway cart.

Tension snapped through me as he lifted the towel and I saw an arrangement of gleaming silver metal medical instruments. There were nipple clamps, speculums, metal vibrators and more.

Dr. Ball grabbed the arm of the examination lamp and slid it in low, aiming it between my legs. He turned on the lamp and warmth whispered against my wet pussy.

"You're lubing yourself quite nicely, Jean," Dr. Ball said.

I swallowed and nodded. This was the first time he'd commented on how wet I became when he examined me.

"I'll start with her breasts and work my way down," Dr. Smith said.

Dr. Ball nodded with a tense smirk and Dr. Smith moved to my right side.

"Now, we'll just start the examination, Jean. Just relax and breathe into everything I do, okay?"

I nodded and gasped as he slurped some ointment onto his fingers. Then his hot hands intimately cupped my breasts. I almost bucked off the table as his searing touch sent tingles of shockwaves through my globes.

"It *has* been a while since a man has touched you, hasn't it?" he commented.

I nodded as his fingers began kneading sweet circles around my big pink areolas.

"Beautiful, healthy, full breasts," the doctor commented as a hot line of tingling fire began to burn wonderfully wherever he touched with his ointment. He traced his fingertips across my dusky nipples. They automatically hardened into rock-hard rosebuds.

"It *has* been too long for you," he mumbled. He slipped his hot palms beneath my mounds and tested their weight.

The gentle embrace made me moan. Dr. Smith didn't seem to notice, but Dr. Ball sure did. His luscious lips curled upward into a knowing smile and then his gaze returned to between my widespread legs and to my creaming pussy.

I groaned as Dr. Ball lifted a shiny silver-colored speculum from the tray. He lubed it and then slid it into my vagina. He clamped it open, stretching my vaginal walls until my muscles protested with a tinge of pleasure-pain. Then, he lifted a metal vibrator and slipped it between my thighs, into the speculum and into me. The smooth vibrator was huge, the pressure of the intruder quickly built as he dipped it all the way inside. He turned it on. Sweet electrical pulses zipped along my vaginal muscles and into my lower belly.

My thighs tightened with arousal. My breaths came faster. I was panting as he slid the vibrator in and out of my pussy as if it were a cock. Sweat began to blossom over my forehead. I struggled to close my legs. They wouldn't budge.

Pleasure pounded my pussy and I moaned. I needed release already. Big-time bad.

Dr. Smith began pinching my sensitive nipples with a pair of forceps. Electricity shot through my breasts and erotic images of these two men fucking me began to dance in my head.

This kinky physical exam with *two* doctors touching me was new to me and I liked it, but it sure was leaving me wanting more. Much more.

Dr. Smith ascended to the next level in his exam as he clamped the forceps on my left nipple, leaving it there, stinging my sensitive flesh with pleasure pain. His fingers kneaded and massaged an erotic trail along my stomach, then to my trembling abdomen. His palms smoothed extremely close to my pubic hair before he stopped. He removed his hot hands from me and I exhaled a shuddering breath wishing he would keep going.

"Everything looks great so far, Dr. Ball. Let me check her down below."

Dr. Ball stepped aside and Dr. Smith moved between my restrained legs.

I seemed to feel as if I was drugged with excitement as an erotic flood of sensations washed away any remaining embarrassment of having two men doing the naughty to my naked body. When Dr. Ball removed the vibe and then the speculum, a gush of hot cream escaped me and drenched my inner thighs. Dr. Smith slid the tip of his tongue out between his lips with the appearance of concentration and then he wiggled a couple of his fingers up inside my pussy. I moaned as a flame of lust jolted me and I arched violently against the heat seeking missiles.

"I'm going to give you a prescription for your problem, Jean," Dr. Smith said softly.

A thumb slid against my aching clit making me moan as carnal tremors rocked me. Dr. Smith's other fingers continued to probe inside my creamed opening and I began to react violently, biting my bottom lip in frustration and pushing my hips harder against his hand.

"I'm going to prescribe that you have two men fuck you good and hard, and then call me in the morning and tell me if you feel better."

Chapter Three

Surely I didn't hear him right.

"You mean two aspirin," I gasped as Dr. Smith rubbed my clit harder. My inner thigh muscles tightened. My vagina quivered. Pleasure curled all around me. Wow! He was good!

"No...I mean two men. If you'd prefer, we can administer the prescription right now."

Sweet mercy! I couldn't even answer. My pussy grew white-hot under his intimate touches.

I eagerly nodded, unable to believe my luck. I was a hard-working waitress and worked plenty of double shifts to meet my rent and other obligations, and I had no time for relationships. Coming here and getting Dr. Ball's controversial stress release was something I really looked forward to. Now, with having two doctors administering the medication I needed, I had something even more to look forward to.

Two doctors, taking me.

"First, I must inspect how wide you are," Dr. Smith said.

"How...wide?" I asked not understanding his question and not quite believing I was actually going to go through with this.

The doctor's finger slipped out of my vagina and I sighed in frustration. I wanted him touching me more.

"Please don't stop," I begged him.

His blue eyes sparkled. "Oh, I'm not." He grabbed a tube off the tray and generously lubed all his fingers.

What was he doing?

I was about to ask that question when he stepped between my legs again. I tensed as a lubed finger slid against my ass. A little gentle prodding and his digit was inside me, exploring my hole.

Another finger slipped inside and my ass seared wonderfully as he moved around, loosening my tight muscles. When yet a third finger

16

entered my hole, my breaths were coming in aroused gasps between my parted lips.

"She's very tight," he muttered to Dr. Ball, who was now standing behind and to the right of Dr. Smith. I hadn't even noticed he'd moved away.

"She'll be fine. I'm sure her heart is strong enough to take the stress of me impaling her."

My heart? Stress? Impaling me?

That's when I noticed Dr. Ball was now totally and gloriously naked. Dr. Smith removed his fingers from my pussy and lowered the end of the bed, allowing Dr. Ball intimate access to me. I inhaled an aroused breath as his swollen shaft pressed past my tight sphincter, his solid flesh sliding into my tightening ass.

We both groaned wildly. He stopped, and then pushed harder. Burning pleasure-pain gripped me as he continued to deepen his impalement. Overwhelming desire ripped through my ass as he sunk his straining erection even deeper. My anal muscles reacted brutally, coiling around his hard long penis as his entire length filled my hole quite deliciously.

I love the feeling of the restraints and of being touched, and of being pierced by a penis. I enjoyed this incredible immense fullness of a big cock burrowing into my rear. I loved the rough way his hands gripped my hips until it hurt.

He pushed harder and I cried out as his powerful thrust created a ripple of ecstasy along tender nerve endings.

"She's on birth control?" Dr. Smith asked.

Dr. Ball groaned a yes.

Dr. Smith had undressed and I was barely aware of him as he unclamped the forceps from my aching nipple and then climbed on top of the examination table.

It was surreal. Like how could a grown man be able to climb up onto the table so quickly and easily? But he did. He held his giant erection in his hands. His mushroom-shaped cockhead flared a deep purple. Blue veins interwove along the length of what appeared to be a nine-inch shaft.

I swallowed at the carnal sight. He was going to penetrate me with *that*. With Dr. Ball's cock already deep inside my ass.

My goodness. It was the stuff my late-night naughty fantasies were all about, with well-hung men tying me down and fucking me.

When Dr. Smith stood above me on the table with both his feet planted beside my restrained arms, I stared straight up at his big pulsing penis and taut swollen testicles. Dr. Smith squatted in front of Dr. Ball, who kept my ass impaled. Then Dr. Smith maneuvered his muscular body on top of me. I moaned as his big cock sank deep into my trembling, tight vagina. His hips crashed against mine, his belly aligned on top of my belly and his big chest squashed my breasts.

I noticed the awkward way Dr. Smith had cast his legs out off the bed and against the outside of Dr. Ball's hips. Then Dr. Ball quickly withdrew and sunk into my ass again. The movement sent Dr. Smith's cock deeper into my vagina.

I cried out and arched against Dr. Smith, whose mouth quickly clamped over mine in a mind-numbing kiss, cutting off my cries.

Any uncertainty I might have had lingering about this unusual prescription vanished when the two doctors withdrew their shafts at the same time and then began a quick double penetration into my wet cunt and well-lubed ass.

Their pistoning rhythm had me crying out from the line of erotic fire zapping deep into my pussy.

"So goddamn beautiful," Dr. Ball ground out. His eyes were scrunched tight. His hot breath fanned my face.

"So goddamn tight," Dr. Smith said against my mouth as he broke the kiss for a second and then his lips fused over mine again.

Their thrusts were slow and torturous and had me groaning from the sheer intensity of double penetration. Soon the thrusts became faster. Deeper.

Hotter. Quicker.

I could feel the doctors' swollen penises sliding in and out of me. My eager cunt and ass muscles clenched around the thick intruders.

All three of us were moaning and I became dazed at the intensity of how both men pulsed inside my two channels. Shards of white lightning blazed and sliced deep.

The doctors were stroking and plunging, their grunts of arousal loud and sensual. I tried to hold their erections inside me with my spasming muscles as they kept withdrawing their hot, slippery organs of lust.

A puff of air and whimpers escaped my lips as the two magical doctors continued to probe into me with their delicious cocks, exploring boldly, thrusting deeply.

Jagged shards of sweet contractions exploded through me. I thrashed my head sideways as I rotated my hips as best I could against the two men who double-penetrated me.

I shivered beneath them.

Panted. Moved hard against the sensual explosions that burst into me. Their hot throbbing shafts continued to impale me. Thrusting in and out, the seductive spirals of carnal lust crashing into me over and over again.

It was exquisite. Blindly beautiful.

The two doctors were groaning and grunting and hammering their gorgeous cocks into me so violently I felt as if I my mind would splinter beneath the pleasure.

I surged under climaxes and the pleasure shattered over me.

Soon their hot juices jet into my steaming channels as they reached their own sexual thresholds.

"Well, how did you enjoy the prescription? Did it work for you?" Dr. Smith asked many minutes later after the two doctors had withdrawn from my sweaty and quivering body.

I lay stunned, not believing how satisfied I felt.

"It's just what the doctor ordered," I answered breathlessly. I smiled at both of them as Dr. Ball released me from my restraints.

Both doctors grinned back at me and they slipped on their clothes.

"Remember," Dr. Smith said. "Call the doctor in the morning and tell him how you are feeling and then we can set up a follow-up appointment for tomorrow evening."

Oh yes! *For sure!*

I eagerly nodded and thanked them for their immense pleasure abilities.

"That's what doctors are for," Dr. Smith chuckled and they both slipped out the door leaving me to agree with the saying, "Sex every day keeps the doctor away."

The End

Taken by Two Bikers

Jasmine Black

When waitress Zoe Miller's car breaks down late one night on a deserted road, she's thankful her biker ex-boyfriend and his best friend come to her rescue...in more ways than one!

Taken by Two Bikers
By Jasmine Black

Chapter One

"No! No! No!" I shouted with frustration and pounded my fist on the steering wheel as the red gas gauge light flickered and then died on my dashboard. My heart sank as the car stalled right there in the middle of the desolate road.

Shoot! I'd hoped I could make it home — or at the very least to the garage — before I ran out of gas, but it seemed luck wasn't on my side tonight. I'd worked a double shift as a waitress at a truck stop in the next town and I was so tired I could barely see straight. That stupid gas light always popped off and on. It had a glitch and I'd hoped the light was just screwing with me tonight. Well, it seemed it did screw me over and good.

I looked out at the blackness and shivered as the cold October air crept into the car. Midnight had come and gone and there was literally no one living along this stretch of farmland. No way to get help. I'd left my cell at home this morning as the battery had died.

Man! Of all times for the car to run out of gas. Why now?

No use crying over it. I could either stay here and sleep until someone came along or get out and walk the five or so miles in my skimpy waitress outfit to get to the garage my ex-boyfriend owned and lived in a room at the back.

Just thinking of Gil chased the chill right out of me. That man had a sexy way about him and I still wondered why I'd broken up with him. Oh yeah, now I remembered. He'd wanted to *share* me with other guys. Sharing turned him on.

I'd told him where he could stick that proposition, and I'd regretted breaking up with him ever since. The more I'd thought about his sharing idea, the more I'd liked it. But pride kept me away from him. I wasn't going to go begging to get back into his bed.

I sighed and closed my eyes. And waited.

I had almost fallen asleep when I heard the distinct rumble of motorcycle engines. I'd been around Gil long enough to recognize the sound of bikes because he was a biker himself. When I opened my eyes, two motorcycles were almost upon my car.

Nervousness wrapped around me. I was alone. And there were two bikers. Big guys, dressed in black leather and black helmets, their faces hidden behind dark visors.

I swallowed and my heart began to pound as they slowed and came to a stop directly beside my car.

Shit.

They switched off their engines and turned to look at me. Panic wrapped around me. They looked dangerous. I wanted to get out of the car and run into the nearby fields and hide. The biker closest to me got off his bike, came over to the driver side of my car, and tapped on the window with his leather gloved finger.

I shook my head. No way was I going to open the window. No freaking way.

He straightened and then for a long minute just stared up the road. I tensed as he reached up and unbuckled his helmet.

Oh no. These guys meant business. They knew I was alone. They could do whatever they wanted to me. My heart felt as if it were about to explode as I awaited his next move.

He lifted the helmet off his head and when I saw the familiar shaggy hair, I breathed a sigh of relief.

Gil. My hero.

I opened the door and he frowned.

"What in hell are you doing out here all alone?" he growled.

"Ran out of gas. I need a fill-up."

He groaned and the erotic sound made me aware of how he took my meaning. My heart began to pound again and my breathing was suddenly too shallow.

"It's too late for you to be out. Something could have happened, Zoe."

"Well, maybe I wanted something to happen," I teased.

The way he tensed and the way his gaze darkened with lust led me to believe he was taking my comments very seriously.

The other biker shifted uneasily on his bike. For a moment, I'd forgotten he was there. But now I was very aware of both of them. I hadn't been laid since breaking up with Gil several months ago. Since then, I'd played it safe. Too damned safe. Avoiding men. Avoiding sex. Avoiding Gil.

"You better quit toying with me, Beauty, or something *will* happen tonight."

Uh oh, when he called me by my nickname, I knew he was seriously aroused.

I smiled.

He cursed softly.

"Get out of the car. I'll take you somewhere safe, then Joel and I will get some gas out here and bring your car back to you."

Disappointment hit me. Somewhere safe? Since when had Gil gotten so boring?

I grabbed my purse, rolled up my window, got out of my car, and locked it. Gil handed me his extra helmet and I put it on and latched it into place. I waited for him to get on his bike, then I climbed on behind him, straddled the seat, and curled my arms around his waist. Just like old times.

His powerful body felt good against mine. Suddenly I felt safe. The engine roared to life and within seconds, we were cruising down the highway with his friend right behind us.

Chapter Two

It only took about ten minutes until we pulled into the garage. The scents of oil and gas wrapped around me and I realized I'd missed these smells. Missed this place too.

As we all got off the bikes, Gil's friend removed his helmet. I recognized him immediately. Joel was one of Gil's good friends. He was a mechanic who worked for Gil, and as Joel gazed at me, his green eyes were intense with interest.

"Hey, Zoe, long time."

"How's it been? How's your mom and dad?" I asked him. I knew he was really close to his parents and he always enjoyed talking about them.

His face relaxed and his voice grew soft.

"Still living it up in Arizona. They love it there. They've added two rescue dogs to their retirement."

"That's great. I'm glad to hear it."

Joel smiled and went down a hall into a back room where he began rummaging around, most likely for the jerry can.

"So, you want to be serviced, do you?" Gil whispered. He'd come up behind me and I could feel his intense body heat. I'd forgotten how tall and big he was and how protected I felt around him.

"Gil..." I should tell him I'd only been teasing him earlier. But that would be a lie.

"I won't do anything without Joel involved. That's the only way you're tumbling back into my bed," he whispered in a hoarse voice.

Arrogant son of a gun, wasn't he? But the idea of getting it on with Gil *and* Joel excited me.

"Two for the price of one. Not a bad deal," I joked. Gosh, I couldn't believe I was pushing him like this.

To my surprise, he reached out and took my hand. It was firm. He meant business.

"Let's go in back, where we'll have privacy," he said.

I trembled as he pulled me down a narrow hallway where Joel had disappeared moments earlier. We passed walls lined with cubicles that contained car and motorcycle parts and my thoughts whirled. What was I doing? Could I go through with what he wanted? I'd never done anything like this before. I mean, Gil had taken me anally on occasion, but having sex with two men? It was scary sexy.

As we passed Joel, who was coming up the hall with a jerry can, Gil stopped and spoke softly to him.

"Joel, lock up and join us in my bedroom. That's an order."

My tummy hollowed out like I was on a roller coaster as Joel grinned and nodded. His lusty gaze swept over me in a very quick and erotic inspection.

"I like your orders, boss," he said.

Then Gil led me to where he lived.

The room in back still looked cozy. I'd been here plenty of times with Gil. The queen-sized bed with dark-green sheets and matching comforter was all military tight, as he'd been taught while in the Army. There were a couple of unwashed dishes on his kitchenette counter, and his room smelled fresh like vanilla. He had this thing for vanilla-scented candles, which he headed toward on a nearby shelf. He lit several of them.

"Can I get you some coffee?" he asked as he plugged in the coffee machine.

"No, thanks. Keeps me up all night."

"That is the idea."

Gil's white teeth flashed in a sensual grin that made my body hum. In a split second, he'd kicked off his leather boots, removed his leather jacket, gloves, and his white T-shirt exposing his broad, bare chest laced with muscles. He stepped closer to me, and his hands spanned my waist. The heat from his body crashed against me like an inferno and my heart began an uncontrollable pound.

"I've missed you like crazy, Zoe," he whispered. His gaze was so intense it shot shivers through me.

"I missed you too," I whispered back.

Boy, did I ever. My gaze dropped over his corded chest muscles to the crisp dark hair that arrowed beneath the waistband of the tight leather pants he wore. I noticed the prominent bulge between his thighs.

"May I undress you?" he whispered.

Like he needs permission?

"You can do anything you want to me," I replied, surprised at how breathless my voice sounded.

"Why are you suddenly so accommodating, Zoe? You do realize what I'm asking, don't you?" Gil said in an ultra-thick voice. Curiosity twinkled in his eyes.

"I want you, Gil. You and Joel." I meant it too. I wanted to lose myself in their arms tonight. I'd think about reality in the morning.

There wasn't even a flinch of jealousy on Gil's face that I admitted I wanted another man having sex with me. Heck, truth be told, I fantasized about sex with more than one guy many times even before he'd mentioned it.

My co-worker and friend, Jean, who worked with me at the diner, had sex with two doctors whenever she went to their office. Their controversial stress release methods worked wonders for her. Having my car die on me tonight had been stressful, these two guys were going to make me forget all my troubles.

My thoughts snapped to what was happening now as Gil swept his fingers along the side of my breast. The waitress outfit I wore was made of a light material and I could feel the heat of his touch permeating the clothing and melting into my flesh.

I shuddered at his touch.

"You sure are primed, Beauty."

Gil's fingers swept ultra-light across the tight fabric over my chest. He stopped at the lace that held the bodice of my uniform together. With one pull, the string loosened. I wore no bra, mainly because not wearing one accented my breasts, allowing my nipples to be prominent against the cloth. I found it got me more tips from the male customers.

I held my breath as he eased the outfit open, bringing the straps down over my shoulders.

We both inhaled as my breasts sprang free. They were deliciously heavy and getting heavier as Gil stared at them. He licked his bottom lip, leaving a glistening trail.

"So sweet," he whispered.

I trembled as I remembered how much Gil liked to suckle my nipples.

Behind me, the door to room opened. I could hear Joel's heavy breathing as he stepped into the room. To my surprise, Gil moved away and Joel came around to my front.

Oh wow.

Joel was naked. Toned muscles laced his chest and arms. His giant serpent of a shaft was fully erect. The mushroom-shaped head was engorged with blood, the stalk unbelievably thick — it looked like it was almost ten inches. I'd never seen a man so well-hung. A wicked fire ignited deep inside my pussy. I creamed warmly. I wanted him. I wanted both of them. I wanted them thrusting their cocks inside me.

Now.

As if Joel could read my thoughts, he smiled knowingly.

"Easy, girl. Patience. Good things come to those who wait."

I nodded numbly. Joel moved in closer, but not close enough for his shaft to touch me. His breath smelled faintly of beer. His breathing was shallow and labored as his head lowered.

Lightning streaked through me as Joel's mouth covered my erect nipple, sucking me. I threw my head back, inhaling deeply at the forbidden sensations rocking me.

Behind me, Gil grabbed my hands, his fingers intertwining tightly with mine. He brought my arms behind my back, allowing my breasts to thrust forward against Joel's mouth.

Moans and gasps swept past my lips as Gil firmly held my wrists and kissed my neck, while Joel suckled my nipple until pleasure-pain burst through my flesh. Joel reached up and cupped my breasts, massaging and kneading with his fingers, and moving his mouth from one nipple to the other until I was panting and creaming and tossing my head back against Gil.

I whimpered with disbelief. How could I be aroused with another man sucking me?

"No need to be afraid," Gil whispered against my ear. He let go of my hands and then cupped my chin and turned my head toward him. He kissed me hard. His lips smoothed over mine in a heated dance of desire.

I became heady as his mouth plundered my lips. He broke the kiss abruptly, leaving me panting and whimpering at the onslaught of shivers and excitement.

"Have a taste, Joel," Gil growled.

Joel let go of the nipple he'd been pulling on and raised his head. His eyes were dark and full of lust and I closed my eyes as his mouth claimed mine.

Intense heat surged through me.

"You stayed away from us because you were afraid," Gil said as his warm lips kissed a line of fire along my neck.

He was right. The idea of two men taking me had taken a while to sink in, but now the thought of two men impaling me was utterly delicious. All my forbidden fantasies were coming to life. Why not embrace them?

Joel's kiss deepened. His lips were frantic as he sipped my lower lip into his mouth. A sharp prick of pain stabbed through my flesh as he pinched me with his teeth.

SHARED 31

Bastard.

My thoughts spiralled. Anger tinged my pleasure and I kissed him back. I thrust my tongue into his mouth, dueling with his tongue and nipping at his lips with my teeth.

Gil eased my outfit lower, past my hips and down my legs. I stepped out of the uniform. My panties quickly followed. I kicked off my heels too. I stood completely naked in front of both men.

Chapter Three

Joel broke the kiss and gazed down at my nude pussy. He gave out a low growl that shot wicked trembles through me.

"I need her bad," he said in a thick voice. His eyes were heavy-lidded and dark with intent.

The air in Gil's room began to heat up as from behind me came the soft sound of Gil's night dresser drawer sliding open. I knew he kept his condoms and lube there.

"We can do it standing up or lying down," Joel whispered as he caught a condom that Gil tossed him. I trembled at the rip of foil and the slurps of lube.

"Both," I managed to say and fought to breathe. Doubts flared as I watched Joel slide the condom over his huge penis. What in the world was I doing jumping into bed with *two* guys? Shouldn't I be protesting or something? Demanding some sort of respect? I'd been warned by my mother that I shouldn't be letting a guy have his way with me until I had his wedding ring on my finger.

But I didn't really want marriage. I liked my freedom and I liked getting fucked by Gil. Always had. He wasn't the marrying kind, and I knew that getting into the relationship. I'd known too, through rumors, that in the past, he'd shared his women. I suspect it was his naughty dark side that had drawn me to him.

I quaked, as a shard of fear at what I had once thought was an unthinkable thing to do, was suddenly becoming reality.

"Just relax, Beauty," Gil murmured in a hard voice. He was now naked and his erection was angling quickly toward his taut belly.

Their body heat was like fire licking my skin as they moved closer to me. The muscles on Joel's chest and arms flexed as he caressed his penis. I gazed down at the bulging length of his shaft as it neared my pussy. Ribbons of blue veins weaved this way and that heading toward the giant red-flushed cockhead that came closer and closer.

Perspiration sheened across my forehead. My legs trembled. Instinctively, I reached out and wrapped a hand around Joel's shaft. It was hot and hard and jerked against my palm.

Joel cursed beneath his breath. His eyes brightened as I stroked the length of his velvet-encased shaft, exploring his girth and trying to figure out how that steel-hard flesh was going to get into me.

"I've been dying to fuck you from the first time I saw you with Gil, but he wanted to get to know you better before he shared you," Joel murmured. His eyes were intense and glazed with lust. His voice dripped with desperation.

My cunt was sizzling and weeping wet and my legs weakened as his flesh jerked in my hands. I shook as Gil's lubed cockhead nudged against my sphincter. My ass had always been extra sensitive, and this time was no exception. He dipped into my ass, working the lubricant against muscles that gripped him like a glove. He groaned and then sank deeper, driving jolts of pressure-pain into me.

I cried out and tried to move away from his explosive penetration. But his hands seared around my waist pushing between Joel and me, one hand slipping between my thighs, his fingers massaging my sensitive clit. Pain was forgotten and pleasure zapped me.

Oh yes. This is what I need.

Hunger filled me. Tension and pleasure built making me gasp and writhe.

"You belong to us now. All of us," Gil whispered against my ear.

Carnal alarm shuddered through me, and I swallowed back a bout of panic as Gil's cock, thick and steel-hard, pulsed even deeper inside me. His penis was heavy and the pressure up my ass only intensified. Gil stopped massaging my clit, his hands leaving my waist and then Joel pushed my hands off his penis. Quickly, he penetrated my vagina.

The pressure of two shafts sliding into me had me gasping for air.

"Shh, we'll make up for all the lost time," Gil said. He swept my hair up, his fingers twisting into my strands to the point where erotic pain seared my scalp. I shivered into the discomfort, enjoying the pain. Gil held me tight as he kissed and nipped at my neck. His mouth was hot, his lips moist, his teeth sweetly sharp against my flesh.

Both cocks pressed deeper. The pressure was intense as they drove their hard thick columns inside. The dual penetration tightened my muscles and a bout of awareness shot through my pleasure like a torpedo. What had Gil meant by *all of us*?

I sensed he wasn't telling me something. *All of us*. He wanted me with more men than just Joel? Instantly, both men moved harder against me and began a steady, pistoning rhythm.

My senses exploded and I cried out, losing all self-control. I moaned in shock as my muscles clenched and spasmed around the big intruders. This was unlike anything I had ever experienced before. My thoughts disintegrated. My mind was shutting down, my body melting into pleasure. I writhed against them, clenched my fists as they took me. Hard, fast and furious.

Lightning-hot sensations arced through me. Shudders ravished me. Their roughness excited me.

I was sweating, panting, and loving it.

Joel's mouth clamped over mine. His hips thrust faster. I creamed more. Both stroked faster, deeper. I thrashed and moaned and was swept into the orgasm. It went on forever. They kept pumping. Kept me inside the pleasure as it tore through me like a tornado. My muscles locked onto them, sucking their cocks, loving the pleasure-pain of ultra-deep penetrations.

My legs grew weaker as they kept fucking me. I reached up and slapped my hands over Joel's shoulders, holding onto him for strength.

They kept riding me. Faster. Deeper. Their muscular bodies slapping against me. The aroma of sex wafted through the air, mingling with the vanilla-scented candles.

Oh wow! I was going to go insane inside this bliss.

I was in the zone, riding the pleasure, crying out both their names, telling them to keep fucking me. *Harder! Harder!*

Before I knew it, I was keening and convulsing, helpless as they rocked against me. I couldn't escape the pleasure. I was drowning in it. Loving it. It was like air. I needed it. Wanted it.

"More, more," I chanted. My vision darkened. They kept fucking me.

Oh wow. So *beautiful.* I wanted to stay here forever. Forever in bliss.

I didn't know how it happened, but soon I realized I was on my back on the bed. I didn't even remember them climaxing or withdrawing from me or them moving me here. But as my breaths heaved and my eyes opened, Joel was climbing up the bed between my spread legs, while Gil was bringing one of my arms up and to the side. Something soft and leathery lashed my wrist. Restraints.

He was breathing hard as he grabbed my other arm and raised it. He lashed my other wrist. He was making sure I wasn't getting away. Not that I wanted to. They were tying me down. Holding me hostage to their desires.

My pussy creamed hotter, gushing out of me. I *needed* them fucking me again.

I was shaking as Joel's hot breath lashed my ultra-sensitive and engorged clit.

"Very nice, sweet baby. Very nice pussy," Joel whispered. He moved his head downward and I cried out and jerked against the restraints as his intense pleasure licks lashed my clitoris.

"Hey Beauty, we're just getting started," Gil groaned as he climbed on his hands and knees over my upper torso, angling his ultra-long cock toward my mouth.

He'd removed his condom. I knew what he wanted.

Wanted to feel my lips wrapped around his shaft. Nothing between us.

Between my thighs, Joel lashed my clit until I was convulsing and moaning. Quickly, he thrust a finger inside my sopping vagina, then a second, and a third. He began pumping his fingers into me. Hard, fast, deep.

Heat uncoiled and convulsive sensations exploded through me. I lost control, drowning in ecstasy once again. I panted into the pleasure and Gil pressed his cockhead into my mouth and I eagerly sucked. I loved his groans and how his cock pulsed and jerked in a dance against my lips.

That I was orgasming and pleasuring Gil at the same time shot shards of extreme happiness through me.

Yeah, I must be crazy. Crazy for doing this. For letting this happen.

But it felt right having a man at my pussy and another man fucking my mouth. It felt damned good too.

I took more of Gil's rigid flesh into my mouth. I caressed his length with my tongue and nipped his flesh with my teeth. He moaned with appreciation and began thrusting. My lips locked around his plunging flesh and I made love to his cock.

His cock tightened, jerked and he cried out as hot jets spurted down my throat.

Yeah, these two guys were keepers.

Somewhere in the distance, I heard the rumble of a motorcycle.

"That would be one of my brothers," Gil growled as he slipped his limp shaft from my quivering mouth. He made no move to unleash the wrist restraints. Instead, he left me on the bed, with Joel's mouth leisurely exploring my pussy while Gil poured himself a coffee.

He winked at me.

"Did I mention my oldest brother was coming over to join us?"

Oh mercy. *Three* bikers fucking me? The idea of having *three* men taking turns with me while being tied down, spun another jolt of desire through me. I was captured in a web of ménage and I knew there was no turning back.

The End

Taken By Two Billionaires

Jasmine Black

Jill has always been warned that her gambling lifestyle would get her into trouble. And now *she's in trouble*.

She's lost a poker game to two very sexy billionaires and they want *her* as their winnings.

They'll to do her whatever they wish...for an entire year.

On her way to her new life in Italy, while in a white stretch limo, Franco and Gianni will show Jill exactly what it means *to be won* by two billionaires.

Taken By Two Billionaires
Jasmine Black

Notes

This is a work of fiction. Characters, places, settings, and events presented in this book are purely of the author's imagination and bear no resemblance to any actual person, living or dead or to any actual events, places, and/or settings.

Chapter One

You belong to us now.

One of the two Italian billionaire brothers who'd won me in a poker game last week had said those exact words a few moments earlier when he'd shown up at my luxury Las Vegas hotel room to pick up his winnings.

Me.

The two men had given me a week to prepare myself. They'd given me a luxurious suite in a hotel that they owned. Heaven knew I'd needed the extra time alone to wrap my head around what had happened.

I still hadn't fully processed the loss of my freedom and despite Franco's impatience, he'd been nice enough to take my luggage to the limo while I used my bathroom one final time so I could make sure my makeup and my hair were perfect. I stared at myself in the mirror.

I looked...bedroomy breathy. I'd splashed a dash of bright red lipstick across my lips, put on the black leather lace slave collar with matching wrist cuffs, stepped into a pair of white sandals and wore a sheer flared frost-white dress with a gold top to bottom zipper down the front. The sandals, dress and naughty accessories had been laid out on my bed this morning by the maid who'd given me specific instructions that I was to wear no bra, no panties and no butt plug when I was picked up.

Removing the plug had left me craving for my ass to be filled again. But I tried to ignore the emptiness as I looked in the mirror. I had to admit the dress hugged my figure like a glove. The material smoothed over the curves of my breasts. My nipples were hard points and the dark areoles shimmered through the fine material of the dress. It really looked sharp. Normally, I wouldn't wear something so provocative. But my life wasn't in my hands anymore. That's the way it was in the world of gambling. You lose some. You win some.

My fingers shook as I pressed a stray strand of my shoulder length brown hair back into place behind my ear. My cheeks were flushed a pretty pink and my blue eyes glittered with excitement, despite the circumstances.

I'd always been warned that my gambling habit would get me into trouble, I'd just never imagined it would get *me* into trouble. Why in the world had I ever agreed to put *myself* up as collateral if I lost the poker game? Maybe because I'd been flirting with those two billionaires for over a year now during poker games. I'd always managed to distract them and won plenty of money. This time I'd been so sure I'd win. I'd even smiled when a naughty voice at the back of my thoughts teased me by saying that win or lose, I'd still win with these two hotties in my bed.

But I hadn't won the game and now I was to be taken by two billionaires whom I'd heard loved to share their women with each other and other billionaires.

A knock came at the bathroom door, making me jump.

"The limo is here and it's time to go. Are you fully prepared? " Franco Minnigetti called from the other side of the door. His voice was commanding and edged with a bit of excitement.

Fully prepared as in that huge butt plug removed, I'm sure he meant. I had made it to the largest of four plugs that had been left for me to prepare myself. I couldn't wait to experience what these two men were going to do to me while a pleasure slave to them for a full year.

"Yes. Be right out," I answered.

Gosh, my voice sounded too husky. I needed to calm down or they'd think I had actually wanted to lose the game on purpose just so I could be with them. I still hadn't explained to my family and my boyfriend what had happened. A new boyfriend, whom I hadn't even slept with, was demanding an explanation as to why I wouldn't be back into the country for a year. How could I tell him I was going off with two men? Men who'd be taking me over and over again, even against my will as had been stated before the poker game had begun. I'd been warned about what would happen. I hadn't taken them seriously. However looking back at it, I should have been tipped off by their smug looks during the card game.

My legs trembled as I opened the bathroom door. My heart galloped at a mad pace as I gazed up at him. He was tall. Six feet four, to my five feet five. His black hair was combed back off his forehead, his face was freshly shaven and he smelled like an expensive ice wine. Sweet and sexy. His square chin had a deep cleft, his nose was a bit hawkish, but his wide smile made my insides quiver in a really nice way.

When he extended his hand, any thoughts of family and boyfriend vanished. I pressed my palm against his and he squeezed my fingers gently. His hand was warm yet firm.

"You look beautiful. Not to worry, *cara*. We will be gentle with you. At first."

I nodded shakily and he pulled me along with him out of my first-floor hotel room, down the lavish hall adorned with a myriad of crystal chandeliers and outside the building where a shiny white stretch limousine sparkled beneath the early October Las Vegas sunshine.

A female chauffeur, dressed in a black hat, black pant suit with light blue tie and wearing absolutely no blouse or shirt beneath, opened the furthest rear side door for me. I didn't miss the knowing grin on her face as I passed her and got into the limo.

Despite my increasing nervousness, I admired the interior of the vehicle. Everything was porcelain-white. And I mean everything. The floor, seats, walls, and windows were white but I could clearly see outside, yet I had not been able to see inside as I'd approached the vehicle.

Sitting on the back seat, was the other billionaire. Gianni. He wore a snappy looking black suit and blue tie and he sat with his legs crossed, a flute of pink champagne in his left hand. He was dipping a luscious looking partially chocolate covered cantaloupe chunk into his mouth.

His well-manicured fingers dripped with the chocolate and juice from the fruit.

He didn't say a word as his lips sucked on his cantaloupe and he motioned me with a nod of his head to take a seat beside him. A seat that matched the color of my dress and it was exactly at that moment that it hit me with a sense of disappointment.

The theme of white. My white dress. I was an object for them. A plaything for these two billionaires.

I sighed and fought back a bite of panic. I would need to keep my cool until I got used to life at the whim of the wealthy.

He smelled just as nice as his brother and looked similar, with black hair, that hawkish nose, and chiseled chin with a cleft. But his hair was longer and his eyes were darker and more intense as he gazed at me.

Across from where we sat was a small ivory colored flat screen television with some sort of stock market channel. I knew that's how they both had become billionaires. Using the stock market.

"She's the best win we've ever had, wouldn't you say, brother?" Franco chuckled as a moment later he plopped into the seat on my other side.

"She is beautiful to look at with the dress on, yes, but how is the rest of her? How will she be when she is speared by the two of us?" Gianna answered.

My breath halted at the picture he created in my mind. Impaled by the two of them? A ménage? They were talking about me as if I weren't even here. Something like this had never happened to me before and I had no idea what I should say. Should I remind them I was here? Or keep my mouth shut? I decided to remain silent and see how it all played out.

Gianni nodded to the small table in front of us. Wow. I hadn't even noticed the colorful arrangement of food laid out on shiny gold plates on a pristine white cloth. Pastries had been drizzled with chocolate and sprinkled with edible gold leaf. There were fruits I'd never seen before too. Golden-yellow fruit in the shape of a star. Another, a bright yellow melon with horns had been split open and the interior was a lush green fruit-flesh.

"Are you hungry, *cara*? Of course you are. And so are we. You are after all our breakfast." Before I knew what was happening Franco leaned over, his confident fingers touching the golden tab of my dress zipper and pulling it assuredly down to my waist.

My lower belly quivered as one of his hands slid inside. He cupped my left breast with a warm hand and popped my breast out for them both to see. Then Gianni dipped his hand inside and lifted out my other breast. Shock rolled through me.

Mercy me, these men moved fast.

Chapter Two

Their breaths quickened with excitement. My nipples hardened as they stared, their smiles hungry. I squirmed uneasily as my breasts heaved in front of their view. Without a word they let go of my breasts and began to place fruit onto a pristine gold plate. I could barely breathe as I sat there. My breasts were bared to them and they casually helped themselves to breakfast? At the front of the limo, the driver was watching us in her rear-view mirror, an amused smirk on her face.

How embarrassing.

Should I cover myself up? I made a move to do so, but Gianna shook his head.

"No, you will allow us to do what we wish. That was the understanding. I will tell you this only one time. Once a garment is removed, you will leave it off until we order otherwise. We own you now as per our agreement. Understood?"

I nodded jerkily, my cheeks warmed and I was surprised that I was creaming warmly at his instruction.

"Now, since you did wrong, you will be punished in order so you do not forget," Gianni's voice had dropped to a soft whisper. I blinked with surprise. *Punish me*?

My heart pounded against my chest as Franco delicately placed a food-laden plate back onto the table. He gazed up at the ceiling of the limo behind me.

"Lift your arms up," Franco said and nodded for me to look up behind me.

I did and caught my breath as I spied a couple of foot long gold chains dangling from the top of the rear window.

"If you hesitate your punishment will be much worse," Gianni said. His voice sounded hoarse. Aroused? From the corner of my eye I noticed how his cock tented his black pants.

Oh my goodness. This was turning him *on*? What had I gotten myself into? For a split second a burst of panic bit me. If punishing me excited them, what will they make me endure? I thought of escape and then my tummy hollowed out as I realized there were no door handles on the inside of the limo. And the limo was already moving.

Shit!

"Up with the arms, *cara*. You gave us your word. Or...is your word not good?" Franco said in a cool voice that sent shivers racing down my spine. To my horror the thought of disappointing them slashed a blade of guilt into me.

"My word is as solid as the gold on your watches or your plates," I reassured.

If it got around I didn't honor my debts, no one would play with me again. I was a professional gambler and I needed to keep my reputation intact. I had to do what they said. I was trapped and at my own doing. I needed to suck it up.

Nervous, I lifted my arms and noticed how my breasts poked boldly out at the two men. Their gazes latched onto my mounds and Franco snapped the chains to the fluff-lined cuffs around my wrists. I pulled at the restraints to test their security but the cuffs held me firm.

My tummy hollowed out with a tinge of fear and of incredible awareness. I also suddenly noticed that toward the front area of the limousine there was a big bed laden with white sheets.

A bed? In a limo? They were going to take me right here?

"Why so trembly? As my brother said earlier, *you* are our breakfast," Gianni purred.

Yes, Franco *had* said that. I'd forgotten due to being so quickly groped.

He leaned over and grabbed a bagel from one of the gold plates. Using a gold knife he sliced the bagel in half and then began to liberally smear a creamy-like substance onto the bread, then topped it.

"I'm sure I will be as delicious as your fruit," I replied. I had to appear cool and confident. The last thing I wanted was for them to see me rattled and insecure.

Inside, I quivered with nervousness and held my breath as Franco lifted a ping pong sized, burgundy-colored fruit from the plate and pressed it against my lips. It smelled sweet.

"Take a bite. These grapes are a favorite of mine. Just like you are," he whispered.

I opened my mouth and sunk my teeth into the firm flesh. Sweetness exploded against my taste buds. Some of the fruit juice dribbled down the sides of my lips, but most of it went into my dry mouth. I swallowed quickly, making love to the flavor with my throat. I waited for him to give me another bite. He didn't.

Disappointment made me whimper. He smiled. The tip of his red tongue peeked between his lips in concentration and he lowered the fruit toward my left breast. I gasped as he pressed the bitten off part and rubbed it over my left nipple, using the large grape like an orange squeezer. Cool sticky juice dripped all over my flesh. Then he lowered his head and I bit my bottom lip to prevent from crying out as he sucked my left nipple between his lips.

"Ahhh, very yummy, no brother?" Gianni chuckled as he watched his brother and then grinned at me.

I exhaled a sharp breath and tugged against the restraints as Franco's teeth began an erotic nibble on my nipple.

Gianni pressed a sweet, scented bagel to my mouth. I took a bite and flavor burst over my taste buds. I couldn't stop from moaning at the delicious taste.

"Good?" Gianni asked.

I nodded. He gave me several more bites and I struggled to savor the taste while Franco leisurely licked my areole and laved my nipple with his tongue.

"The bagel is topped with goji-berry infused with Riesling jelly, a splash of Swiss chocolate and a liberal amount of Italian white truffle cream cheese," he whispered.

"It's delicious." I opened my mouth hoping for more. I needed that sweet taste in my mouth. It was *that* good. He allowed me another bite before pulling the bagel away.

"They grow the white truffle fungus underground on Alba, an island we live on in Italy. That is where we will be taking you. The fungi's pheromone-like odor is considered an aphrodisiac. One bite and you are hooked."

"I'll say," I replied. I craved another bite of that truffle filling.

"Here, a sip of this." He lifted a flute filled with what I perceived was orange juice. The rim was colored with a blue sugar-looking substance and blue sugar cubes floated in the pristine orange liquid. When I took a liberal sip, my taste buds were awash once again with flavor.

"What is it?" I asked, trying like hell to ignore the eager mouth sucking at my breast. But by now I was trembling even more and my senses were heightening.

"It's our own unique blend. In this drink we pour blanc de blanc all Chardonnay French champagne, mix with freshly squeezed ripe orange juice, ice cubes, blue sugar cubes, rose petal nectar, apricot chunks with a touch of blue sugar around the rim. Good?"

"More?" I asked. I wanted to experience another splash of flavor, if only to try to not squirm on the seat while Franco now cupped my breast and was sucking quite intensely, the sweet bite of pain making me cream.

I inhaled softly as Gianni placed a dollop of that truffle cream cheese on my nipple and quickly lowered his head over my breast. His lips parted and he sucked my nipple into his mouth. He began nibbling in the same intoxicating way as Franco.

A desperate ache swept into my pussy. My ass clenched. I whimpered in surprise at my reaction.

Both men moaned around my nipples. Their hands were firm as they kneaded my breasts and when I tried to clench my legs together, Franco reached down and slipped his hand between my thighs.

"Open wide," he muttered around my nipple and blinked up at me. I did it, without so much as a thought.

Wow, they really had me at their mercy and so quickly. How had I been so easily tamed?

I groaned as a finger slid into my creaming pussy. My vagina clenched tightly around him. We both gasped at the intensity.

"Very nice," Gianni whispered. Lust flashed over his face.

I stiffened as he slipped a second finger inside of me and at the same time he let go of my nipple. With his other hand he unzipped his pant zipper and brought out his cock.

Chapter Three

I blinked with disbelief at the size. He was very big. His shaft was flushed a dark purple and webs of veins interlaced the length. A kinky shiver coursed through me as I noted his erection as being much bigger than that last plug they'd had me use while I'd stayed at the hotel.

I creamed as I imagined myself fighting the restraints as he sunk his cock into me.

Oh boy, being held captive was turning me on. Big time.

He smiled, obviously feeling the quivering of my pussy muscles around his fingers and the wetness of my arousal. He withdrew.

I watched him warily as he nudged Franco, who, without letting go of my tit, moved over to the side allowing Gianni to drop to his knees to the floor in front of me.

I started breathing way too fast as Gianni dipped his fingers into the dish of white truffle, brought his fingers between my thighs and liberally smeared the cool delicacy over my labia, then he began erotically rubbing the truffle over my sensitive clit.

Instantly sensations flared hot and wickedly delicious.

"Feel good, no?"

I nodded jerkily and sucked air as pleasure sunk into me. I began to rock my hips, melting into the exquisite arousal he was creating and then tried to squeeze my thighs together. Anger flared in Gianni's eyes. I froze, instantly realizing I'd done something he didn't like.

Quickly he grabbed my knees and held them apart. He shook his head at me, admonishing me with his dark look.

"I do not wish for you to come!"

He nudged his brother, whose eyes popped open with surprise at being disturbed. He stared dreamily at Gianni, as if he'd been in some fantasy world, instead of right here furiously sucking on my nipple.

"Hold her legs open for me!" Gianni demanded. Desperation etched his voice as he stared at my pussy.

51

Involuntarily I continued to undulate my hips. I'd already lost my self-control. That cream he'd spread over my intimate parts made me crave stimulation.

My breast shuddered as Franco let go of my nipple. He swore softly beneath his breath as from a compartment beneath my seat, he withdrew a gold two-inch thick and eighteen-inch-long metal thigh spreader with a black leather thigh cuff dangling from each end.

Oh wow, these guys took their dominance seriously. In a flash, he placed the spreader between my legs and snapped a cuff firmly around each of my thighs. I tried to close my legs, but the spreader only allowed slight movement. I was open and vulnerable to them, whether I wanted to be or not.

Damn!

Gianni's cock had grown even more during the brief interlude. It thrust out from between his open pants like a serpent. The purple color had vanished. His rigid flesh was flushed a very angry red. Something sizzled like fire deep inside my pussy. I wanted him thrusting *that* huge erection deep into me.

I gasped and arched my back as Franco returned to my other breast and latched his hot lips over my pert nipple. His eyes closed and he began a rough suck that had me wiggling on the seat, pulling against the restraints and eagerly waiting for Gianni to take me.

He didn't.

"You do not come until I tell you to. If you do then your punishment will be severe. Understood?"

What? Was he crazy? Gosh, I'd heard about men who wanted to dominate to the point where their women orgasmed only when she was told. Was he that kind of man too? He didn't wait for my answer.

Tension zipped through me as he slid his hands up along the insides of my quivering thighs. His touch was light as he made his way toward my pussy.

He was grinning at me. Obviously, he enjoyed my torment. He smiled nice. He had a beautiful mouth. Soft-looking and lush red lips.

I gasped as Franco bit my nipple. Sharp pain was quickly soothed as he laved my flesh with his tongue. He massaged my breasts with a rough touch. I enjoyed it.

My belly clenched as Gianni's fingers held my pussy lips. He spread them open. Sparkles of appreciation glowed in his eyes as he stared between my thighs. Over his shoulder, I noticed the female driver was casting quick glances in her rear-view mirror. Her gaze was tight, her eyes nearly black as she watched us.

Suddenly a white partition slid up from behind the seat she sat in. It slid into place blocking us from her view.

"Disregard her. She is one of my many female slaves. I won her from her husband in a secret card game in Dubai. She is allowed to watch us play but only to a point," he said as he looked at me.

"You have a beautiful pussy. Like a flower. With velvety petals and a splash of dew which I ache to lick."

Hunger for him to do just that made me moan with anticipation. The need to climax was unbelievably great.

He moved his hands away and sunk the fingers from both of his hands into the truffle cream. He brought his hands toward me, and then smeared the cream liberally over my pussy lips, dipping some into my vagina, and slurping it over my aching clit.

Leisurely he rubbed my clitoris and watched my face. My fingers clenched with frustration. I tried to keep my expression impassive but it was hard. Way too hard as sensations ripped through me. His rubbing increased on my clitoris. I started perspiring and panting, trying hard not to come.

"Now, it is time for my breakfast," he muttered.

I whimpered as he dipped his head to between my thighs. I could barely keep my eyes open as his fingers pulled my labia apart. Need roared through me. I began to whimper my distress.

The sight of his head between my thighs made me want to come. Bad. But he'd said not to. I shook my head in disbelief. Why was I so easily accepting his dominance?

His hot breath caressed my pussy and my inner thighs clenched.

"I want to suck your cream from your body. Feed me your nourishment. You may come when you wish," he whispered.

I could come? My thoughts whirled in disbelief. Had he said that I could come or had I imagined it? A split second later, his entire mouth melted over my vaginal opening. When he thrust his tongue into my vagina, I exploded.

My thighs tightened as hot spirals of pleasure snapped through me. I was out of control. Way out of control as I bucked and struggled against my wrist restraints and the thigh spreader.

I fought for breath as wicked waves of arousal swallowed me. I rode the shudders and convulsed. To my surprise, a hot firm mouth slid against my lips.

Franco. It had to be him because he wasn't sucking on my tit anymore, but his hands were roving over my breasts. He was plumping them and squeezing. His tongue thrust into my mouth and dueled with my tongue. I boldly met his every stroke.

Gianni's tongue was pistoning into my creaming vagina like a miniature cock. I gushed with wetness and he eagerly sucked, making me come over and over until I was so weak and spent I couldn't even keen anymore. Hell, I hadn't even realized I had been keening.

"Get her onto the bed," Franco growled as he broke the kiss and panted against my ear.

Gianni didn't reply but stopped slurping from me. His harsh breath snapped through the air.

I sat on the seat, my body drenched in perspiration and seared with pleasure. I couldn't open my eyes, but I did hear the rustling of clothing as they undressed. Then my wrists were free and my thighs too.

Gianni grabbed one of my arms and Franco my other one. My shoulders and thighs were sore from the restraints and I could barely move but the men transferred me quickly around the table and onto the soft bed. The fluffy mattress beneath me was heaven compared to the leather seat which had rubbed at my bare ass while I'd squirmed beneath Gianni's sensual assault on my pussy.

Two sets of possessive and confident hot hands began roving all over my tender flesh. They pinched and slapped my breasts and pussy until sensations sizzled through me. I cried out at how aroused I was once again. I managed to open my eyes and gazed up to find Gianni and Franco both leaning over the right side of the bed.

My breath caught. Their eyes were dark with lust. Their mouths red from loving me. Both men were naked. The rich life certainly agreed with them. They were physically fit and tanned muscles laced every square inch of their bodies. They looked powerful. Strong enough to hold me down when they took me.

I creamed as I spied their prominent erections. Both cocks were immense. Thick and solid, their swollen lengths cobwebbed with pulsing blue veins. I was impressed but scared at the same time. How in the world would both of *those* fit into me?

I shuddered as Franco's hands slipped between my thighs. Automatically I spread my legs.

"That's what we want. Submissive. I knew you would be one," Franco murmured.

"No coming, until we say. Remember our instructions," Gianni growled as his rough fingers pinched both my nipples at the same time.

I yelped but dared not move to stop him. I knew my place now.

Normally a comment like that would insult me. I'd fight back saying I was no man's slave. But in the intimate way they handled me, their touches arousing and caressing, I couldn't even form any words to protest.

Instead, I whimpered. I was needy, desperate to be double-penetrated. My cunt was wet and my ass was clenching.

Both of them were breathing hard now. Harder than me. I felt myself being turned to my left side. Franco crawled onto the bed. I felt the harsh slap of his rigid cock hit my hip as he climbed over me. The mattress moved when he lay down behind me. I creamed as I heard the rip of foil from both in front of me and behind me.

Condoms.

I began keening again. Eager. Wanting. The slurp of lube zipped through the air. I listened as awareness powered through me.

They were readying themselves.

Oh God.

My belly was tight, my pussy wet and achy. My ass was clamping. Franco's body was hard as he moved against me. Gianni lifted my leg allowing Franco, his shaft generously lubed, to press his rigid flesh against my sphincter. I tensed.

"Easy, *Mia cara*, easy. Let him inside of you," Gianni prodded softly. He smoothed his palm gently over my forehead as if caressing me. This soft side of him stunned me. I forced myself to relax my ass muscles.

Without warning, Franco plunged his stiff rod deep into my ass. The pressure burn was incredible. I wasn't sure if I liked it or not. I tried to wiggle away from his impalement, but Gianni held my leg high. His other hand stayed firm on my forehead, preventing me from moving away from Franco.

"Shh," Gianni soothed. "Just relax and let him fuck your beautiful ass."

I nodded unable to think. Franco's cock was huge inside me. My ass muscles protested as he withdrew and then quickly slid in again, deeper this time. I creamed. Tried to move away from the powerful thrust. But Gianni continued to hold me firmly in position.

"She is as sweet as I thought," Franco said in a guttural voice against my ear. He sucked on my earlobe and then his hand came around me and he grabbed my breast, his fingers pinching my nipple to give me a sweet pain I enjoyed.

"Now onto your back, sweet," Gianni demanded.

I blinked, unable to comprehend what he'd just said. On my back? With a man's cock buried inside my ass? How?

"We will help," Gianni said.

To my surprise, Gianni pushed on me and Franco held onto my breast as I was pushed back with Franco attached to me. A moment later I was on my back, Franco beneath me, his shaft still impaling my ass and Gianni was climbing over me.

"Exquisite female, Franco," Gianni growled as he came down on me.

Franco grunted and then said. "She is perfection, brother. Her pussy is a tight-fitting glove around my cock. I wish to lay buried inside of her forever."

My eyes widened. Forever?

Gianni must have noticed my surprised expression. He chuckled. "No mind him. He enjoys the pressure of two bodies on top of him. Now you belong to me. To us."

His hard shaft pierced into my vagina in one fast powerful thrust. Franco grunted at the impact, and I cried out as Franco's cock plunged deeper into my ass.

Instinctively I slid my fingers through Gianni's silky hair as his mouth melted over mine, preventing me from crying out again as he withdrew and pistoned into me again and again. I jerked at the rough impalements. Every one of his powerful thrusts, rocked new sensations through me, reigniting sensitized nerve endings. My body was tensing again. My pussy muscles quivering around Gianni's throbbing flesh. My anal muscles clenched like crazy around Franco.

Pleasure raced through me. I needed to come. Bad.

"Tight. She is so very *bellissima* tight," Gianni muttered against my mouth. He kissed me harder until my head was spinning and my body was no longer my own. I belonged to them and they played with me as if I were their sex toy.

I was given no time to think as suddenly I was rolled onto my side once more. I was sandwiched between their hard lengths with both men's shafts buried inside of me. Suddenly they were withdrawing, and then moving into me again.

Their sensual pistoning made me so ready to explode.

"Please!" I gasped as I tore my mouth from Gianni.

"What is it!" he growled as he sipped on my lower lip with such a sensual stroke it made me heady.

"I need to come," I whimpered.

"You will come only after we do, is that understood? It will always be this way. Always after us unless you are told. Understand?"

I nodded. I understood. I needed to make them come. Then I could too. I gyrated my hips, moved my breasts against Gianni with a desperation I'd never experienced before.

Both men chuckled, but I didn't care. I needed satisfaction. I kissed Gianni back, thrusting my tongue into his mouth, demanding his tongue mate with mine. We twirled around each other. My arousal increased. My frenzy and desperation increased. I thrashed and bucked and within seconds both men growled and groaned. Their bodies tensed, their thrusts grew faster, rougher and then both of them exploded.

Hot liquid gushed into my protected openings. I couldn't stand the tension anymore; the pleasure gripped me like a wild storm. Ecstasy slammed into me and I came apart. My mind shattered, breaking into a million colorful pieces. Agonizing arousal flooded me and I was swept into an undertow of convulsions of exquisite proportions.

My old self was lost and I was reborn. I knew I would never be the same again.

The End

Taken by Two Bosses

Jasmine Black

Trapped in the company elevator, receptionist Carina Chantilli is suddenly at the mercy of her two sexy bosses...

Chapter One

Hold the elevator!" I called out as I spied the doors begin to close. I cringed as my voice echoed way too loudly down the empty hallway and I quickly pushed the cart toward the elevator. The cart contained a bag of sample adult toys that Beth from Sales had just left by my desk a few minutes earlier. She'd been in a meeting showing off the toys to prospective purchasers. The meeting had run late and she'd rushed by my desk leaving the cart and toys behind, telling me to return the toys downstairs to Quality Control before I left for the weekend.

I hated it when people took advantage of me like that. Just leaving their work behind and assuming I would pick up after them like I was their slave. It happened a lot with my co-workers. They did it because I had a problem saying no and they knew it.

I was easygoing. A pushover. An idiot.

But right now I just wanted to get the toy samples back to QC. The last thing I needed was for my two bosses to find the bag of adult toys in the reception area. Jokes would fly and my face would get beet red. It did that whenever I got embarrassed. And boy did they ever enjoy teasing me. Thankfully the two men had left for the weekend and I was free of them.

Once the toys were delivered, I'd head home. It was late and I was tired and I was frustrated. I couldn't wait to sink my weary self into a nice tub full of hot water and scented bubbles and do some heavy duty masturbating as I fantasized about my two bosses. In particular about Drew Green and what he'd wanted me to do.

I'd been dating Drew off and on for several months ever since he'd bought the Carnal Toys factory from the former owner.

Recently his best friend, Cooper Endridge had moved to town and Drew had made him a partner of the company. So now I had two bosses, the same old pay and twice the workload.

Oh glory. Fun. Not.

Not too long ago, Drew had brought up a naughty subject that had me questioning my morals. He'd told me he got really turned on when he watched a woman he cared about getting pleasured by another man. He wanted me to have sex with Cooper and himself. That idea had been so shockingly arousing and yet embarrassing too. Mainly because I had secretly fantasized about it already. His request had taken me by such surprise that in an unusual burst of boldness, I had broken off our relationship, telling him that I was not *that* kind of woman. But while doing so, my face had gotten so hot and red, he knew I was lying.

But with Drew being my boss, it was kind of hard to avoid him. Since the break-up, both men had been giving me a hard time in the sexual teasing department. They'd gotten into a habit of asking my opinion on the toys the company made. Sometimes it was one boss, and occasionally the other boss and then sometimes both men together. They would ask my opinion about what I thought about this cock ring sample or if the color of that vibrator was hot or not.

Their constant asking me of my opinion was getting to the point where I was getting hot and bothered. Just earlier this afternoon they'd asked me into one of the conference rooms so they could demonstrate how the red mouth-shaped nipple clamps worked. They'd used a dummy's nipples of course, but boy had I wished they'd put those lip clamps on *my* breasts.

I knew I should remind them I was their receptionist and their asking my opinions about the toys was totally out of my job description, but I really tried hard to avoid confrontation. Hence, why I was pushing a cart with Beth's bag full of toys toward the elevator.

I almost gave up on catching the elevator as the doors continued closing. But a second later, they opened again and I pushed the cart in and followed right in after it.

"Thank you! I am so grateful," I gushed with relief. I'd expected to find Randy, the maintenance man, in the mirrored elevator, but when I looked up, two sets of blue eyes were staring back at me.

"Oh," I muttered as surprise totally shocked me.

Shit! Cooper and Drew were still here. They never stayed late on a Friday night.

Damn, but they sure were cute. They were dressed in neatly pressed white shirts, pressed ties and black slacks. Despite them being here all day, they still looked fresh and clean. I knew they used the company gym and since they both smelled faintly of soap and their hair appeared damp, I realized they'd been working out and had used the showers.

"Good evening, Carina," Cooper said. He was the tallest of the two with feathery dark brown hair. He was so cute I almost came every time I looked at him. I didn't want him to know how taken aback I was at them still being here, so I averted his gaze and prayed my face didn't go red.

I caught my reflection in the mirrored walls of the elevator. I looked wide-eyed scared. Pathetically frightened.

"We would have thought you'd gone home by now, Carina. Way past quitting time," Drew said. He smiled and my tummy did a sweet somersault. His gaze dropped to the toy bag and I noticed his eyes widen. Saw the interest flare in his eyes and a wicked excitement shimmered through me at the forbidden thought of having both men making love to me with the help of some of these toys. I tamped down on that fantasy.

All in good time, Carina. Fantasize in that bathtub full of bubbles.

"Are you taking these toys home to play with them for the weekend?" Drew joked.

I wished I could come back with some smart comment, but instead, my face grew hot. I could see my cheeks growing red. Morbid embarrassment shot through me and I suddenly wished the elevator would simply plummet and let me fall to my death so I wouldn't have to endure their mocking looks.

A sudden jolt from the elevator as it came to an abrupt stop had me crying out as I lost my balance. Both men instantly grabbed me to steady me. Drew held my elbow and Cooper's hand slipped around my waist. Before I knew what was happening the lights above flickered off and then back on again. But the lights were dimmer now. Much dimmer. Instinctively I knew the elevator was on some sort of back-up power.

"Too bad the elevator company isn't up to our standards," Drew mumbled as he pressed the down button several times. Nothing happened. He tried pushing buttons to several floors too. Still nothing.

Oh no, please don't let us be trapped together.

"It died again?" Cooper asked. His breath was liquor scented and caressed my nostrils. I wondered if he'd been drinking or if the smell was some sort of mint he'd eaten. I swallowed as his hot hand branded through the thin blouse I wore.

"Died? Again?" I asked feeling a big wave of despair sweep over me. This was the first I'd heard of a problem with the elevator.

Drew nodded.

"Just this afternoon there was an episode," Drew said. "A few people were trapped in here for about half an hour. The mechanic got it going. Too bad he's gone home."

"What?" I shrieked. It was Friday. The weekend was like here.

No freaking way was this happening. I must be having a nightmare!

"We can't stay here all weekend. We'll die of starvation," I cried.

"My cell phone is in my office," Drew said. "You?" He looked at Cooper and then at me.

Cooper shook his head. "In my office, battery died. It's on my charger."

"Mine is in my purse. On my desk," I answered. Tension ripped through me.

"The emergency phone. Try the phone," Cooper suggested.

Drew nodded, opened a small metal door by the punch buttons, lifted the phone off its cradle and put it to his ear. I watched his face. He frowned.

No! No! No!

"It's ringing, but no answer. Oh, hold on." Relief sliced through me as he suddenly chuckled. "I got an answering machine."

My relief grew as Drew explained into the receiver what had happened. Then he hung up.

"They have an emergency crew for these purposes according to their machine. But it could take some time. Up to twenty-four hours," he said.

"Better than the entire weekend," I mumbled. This just cannot be happening.

"What, Carina? Why wouldn't you like spending a weekend trapped with the two of us?" Cooper asked in a hurt voice. At least I hoped he was kidding. But just looking into his eyes, I got the feeling he was serious. Drew was watching me carefully and my instincts warned me that Drew must have had a conversation or two with Cooper about what he wanted me and Cooper to do.

"Of course I wouldn't mind, but not in an elevator," I blurted. Oh dear, had I just said that? My cheeks grew even hotter. I caught my reflection in the mirror. My face was so flushed red that I suddenly wished I had not worn my favorite short skirt and white blouse. The attire reminded me of the innocent Catholic-girl uniform I used to wear to high school.

"Even in an elevator with a bunch of toys?" Cooper suggested.

Both men stared at me. My mouth went dry as nervousness breathed through me. Surely, they were kidding?

"Um," I stammered. I had no idea what to say. The idea of having sex with two men while trapped in an elevator had just never entered my sexual fantasies.

Drew shook his head and laughed. It was a hearty laugh that bubbled straight up from deep inside his chest.

I relaxed. Oh, okay, they *were* kidding.

"The meeting between the purchasers and Beth this afternoon was a huge success. They gave her big orders for these toys. She left the paperwork on my desk." I might as well bring them up to speed on sales and yep, I was trying to change the subject before my face got so red, the color would become permanent.

I thought they would be pleased with the announcement of sales. But they didn't make note of it.

"Maybe you should give us some demonstrations on how these toys work? Since we seem to have so much time on our hands," Drew said. His voice was a guttural whisper and since I had had sex with him over the months, I knew by his smoky tone he was *not* kidding.

He wanted to have sex here. Now. With Cooper watching? Or her having sex with Cooper?

No way. I couldn't do that. I had already made it clear to Drew that I wasn't that kind of woman. I was easy going but not easy. I'd be mortified if it got around the office that Drew had shared me with Cooper. That was fantasy material. Not reality.

I tensed as Drew wrapped his hand around my right elbow and quickly tugged me against him. His hot body heat wrapped around me and I gulped at the huge bulge pressing against my pussy. I had enjoyed our sexual time together. He had a long and thick penis that had given me intense pleasure, but he had crossed the line suggesting I sleep with his friend.

Cooper remained silent but I could feel his eyes on me as he watched us. His strong masculine scent seeped deep into my lungs, shocking my senses into alert mode. I suddenly felt panicked. I needed to get out of here.

Drew's blue eyes blazed with lust. The hand at my elbow held tighter. Oh, my, he *really* was serious. I swallowed as his other hand lifted and he began to unbutton my blouse.

"Let's start with putting on some nipple clamps," he said in a demanding tone.

No. This cannot be happening.

I looked to Cooper for help. Surely he wouldn't go along with this insanity.

"I'll hold her nice and tight, so she can't run away from us," he said and winked at me. Before I could so much as step away from them, Cooper had moved in behind me. Drew let go of my elbow and Cooper's hands curled steadfast over my shoulders. His hold was firm and his fingers dug almost painfully into my flesh. I couldn't so much as move. I stared at him in the mirror, horrified at this turn of events.

Chapter Two

Cooper gazed back at me and I trembled at the sight of the dark lusty intent flashing in his blue eyes.

Oh my goodness! This truly *was* happening! They were going to have sex with me. Here!

"Just relax, *cara*," Cooper muttered. I jerked as his erection pressed hot and oh so hard against my ass.

Wow, these guys got aroused so quickly.

As Drew continued to unbutton my blouse, his breathing quickened. I heard Cooper's breaths get deeper and raspier. They were enjoying what they were doing to me. I needed to stop this before it got out of control.

"This...shouldn't...um," I began to protest, but then I stopped as Drew tugged my blouse out of my skirt. His hot fingers warmed the flesh of my belly and I couldn't stop the moan at his electrifying touch.

Wow. That felt good.

Um, what had I been about to say?

Heat and embarrassment tore through me as Drew opened my blouse and revealed my lace bra. I watched what happened next, transfixed by Cooper's and my reflection in the mirror, as he held me tight and Drew slipped off my blouse. Then he dropped my bra straps, slowly sliding them over my shoulders and down.

I gasped with shock as my breasts spilled free from the cups. My breasts weren't anything spectacular. Not too big. Not too small. Nothing to be ashamed of. But I had never been in this kind of a situation. Naked in front of two men. With one man restraining me.

My nipples appeared plump and pert. More so than usual. They actually appeared *huge*. Was this possible? Was I actually subconsciously aroused at what was happening to me?

I heard Cooper inhale sharply as he stared. I wanted to cover myself from his heated look, but his hands moved silky smooth down the sides of my arms. Within a second, his fingers intertwined with mine. I found it an endearing gesture. Until he forced my hands behind my back. The new position jutted out my breasts.

"You're right, Drew. She has pretty breasts," Cooper said in a tight voice.

Drew had a satisfied look on his face as he gazed at me. He *had* been discussing me with Cooper. Exactly what he told him?

"By the time we're through with you, sweet Carina, you'll think twice about saying no to me again," Drew said. There was a heavy dominance in his voice. It made me very nervous and I began to tremble.

Is this what this was all about? Payback for my rejection of his idea of my having sex with Cooper?

I tensed as Cooper's fingers tightened around mine. I viewed him in the mirror. His look was dark and forceful. He was not my ally. If anything, he would dominant me until I lost myself. He would be a man who would never accept the word no to sex. A man who would take what he wanted, when he wanted. Like now.

The realization that Cooper wanted me and that maybe I wanted him to take me right here with Drew watching, sent jolts of confusion shooting through me. No, not *this* way. It just was not proper.

My breath caught as Drew lowered his head.

Oh damn. Drew knows my nipples are extra-sensitive. He knows I can't stand the pleasure when his mouth is on me there. In the past he could make me orgasm just by sucking on my breasts in that special way that he did.

"We need...to...ah," I was about to say we needed to talk this through, but my thoughts went absent without leave as Drew's hands roughly cupped my breasts and his hot mouth wrapped around my right nipple. His lips appeared full and puffy and as he sucked, the pressure he created sent pleasure rocking through me. I bucked, tried to get away from the intensity, but Cooper kept me firmly in place.

"Easy," Cooper whispered. "You aren't getting away so you may as well enjoy it."

My pussy creamed at Cooper's dark promise and I closed my eyes, sinking quickly into wicked sensations as Drew's five-o-clock shadow rasped my tender skin. His bristles created a sizzling friction that had me gasping from the passionate current.

I shuddered as his mouth moved skillfully over my flesh. His lips suckled, twisted and pulled. His teasing tongue stalked around my throbbing nipple and his sharp teeth bit none too gently. Sensations snapped through me as Drew continued his sensual assault and I became caught in a vortex, drowning in pleasure and pain.

I almost fell over as Cooper suddenly moved his hard body away and let go of my hands. I could barely register the sound of plastic ripping nearby.

What were they doing? What was happening? I wanted to open my eyes to see, but they were so heavy lidded, I just couldn't. Instead, I reached out and slid my hands against Drew's hips to hold onto him for balance as he moved to my other breast.

I moaned at the pleasure.

"She's really hyper-active responsive. Just as you said," Cooper murmured from somewhere to my right. I sensed appreciation in his voice. Why would he say that? Why the interest?

I jerked and whimpered as something pinched onto my right nipple. Intense pressure and hurt followed. I wanted to get away from the weird sensations, but Drew's mouth and teeth were latched onto my other nipple. I knew I couldn't step away. If I did, I might be injured.

"Nipple clamp," Cooper muttered as if sensing my distress. "You'll wear them no matter how much they hurt. Understand?"

I nodded. My head was jerky. Why was I agreeing?

A naughty throbbing erupted deep inside my pussy. I had a sudden desire to have a cock sliding into my vagina. A need to orgasm.

Instinctively I began to gyrate my hips, moaning as sensations began to erupt from Drew's sucking at my breast. I wanted to follow them. To allow them to blossom and explode.

I groaned, as without warning, Drew let go of my nipple. A sharp pinch and hurt followed there, much as what had happened to my other nipple. Then he moved away. I felt off balance, my pussy sopping wet and weeping for satisfaction.

Blindly, I reached out. Thankfully, someone slid a strong arm around my waist. I liked the tender way I was being held.

I was breathing so heavily; I could barely hear Cooper instructing me to open my eyes. When I obeyed, surprise washed through me as I looked at my reflection.

My eyes appeared vacant as if I weren't even here anymore. My mouth was slightly open, my cheeks were red as roses, and my clamped breasts heaved with my every breath. I realized the clamps were the same type of red lips clamps that the two men had shown me earlier in the day. The ones they'd clamped onto the dummy nipples. I had told Drew and Cooper the clamps looked erotic and in my opinion any woman would be pleased if her man gave them to her. Certainly not in *this* manner.

For a few insane seconds I swore I'd never looked this beautiful before. But then reality crashed in. I was trapped in an elevator with my two bosses and what they were doing to me was highly inappropriate!

I realized Cooper was the one holding me and he was also studying me in the mirror. Maybe looking for my reaction to my breasts being clamped? His face was a dark scowl in direct contradiction to the fact he was nodding his head as if he had come to some sort of conclusion.

"You look beautiful. I must have you presented to me like this all the time, *cara.*" he whispered. "You will wear your nipples clamped beneath your blouses when you come to work. I will look at your breasts whenever I want. Drew will do so whenever I tell him to. And any man I deem to undress you will enjoy you."

Any man? Whenever Cooper wanted to? Whenever he told Drew to? What is he saying? Why would Drew do what Cooper wanted him to do?

I shook my head. What he was saying didn't make sense. This was crazy. He was crazy. I had to get away from them. But how?

My nipples were sore. Aching. Surprisingly aching and not in a bad way. But in a way that I wanted them to be touched tenderly, kissed and caressed gently. But these two men were anything but tender or gentle.

Movement from behind Cooper had me turning my attention to Drew. He'd removed his pants and underwear. He stood naked from his waist down with a huge erection.

I whimpered as I wondered if he was going to just push me up against the wall and take me while Cooper watched? That idea sent a volley of thick heat rushing through me. I shook my head. No, I wouldn't let this happen.

"You've fantasized about us, haven't you, Carina," Cooper murmured. He held me tighter against his side, his head lowered and he kissed my neck. His warm lips were gentle as he moved with butterfly strokes along my flesh. Drew was watching. Hunger tightened his gaze. I noticed him reach down and he began to slap the engorged length of his cock with his hand.

Cooper didn't seem to notice what Drew was doing as he sucked my left earlobe into his mouth. Tingles shot through me.

"Touch yourself. Touch your breasts," Cooper muttered. "I want to watch."

My breaths were quickening with excitement again. I couldn't believe I was actually lifting my hands. I cupped my breasts, squeezed them and looked for approval in Cooper's eyes as he watched me.

I was disappointed when I didn't see his enjoyment.

"Now I want you to remove your skirt," he said softly.

My skirt? Oh no.

"I can't...I." A stern shake to his head had me shutting up.

"Do as I say, *cara*. Never object." Cooper's voice was deep and forceful again. I suddenly had the feeling I'd entered a different world when I'd gotten onto this elevator. A world that I wasn't going to be able to get out of easily. A world where the word "no" simply did not even exist.

Chapter Three

I swallowed and reached around to unsnap my skirt. I should be yelling and screaming, but all I could do was submit to their hot stares. My nipples throbbed with the clamps and my breasts jiggled as I lowered my skirt over my hips and let it drop to the floor.

I hesitated and then dipped my fingers beneath the waistband of my panties.

Cooper nodded for me to continue and I shivered with nervousness as I slipped my panties down. With a shaky foot, I kicked the garments aside.

I stood naked, with just my high heels on, in front of my two bosses.

"Very good, Carina. Very good." I got the feeling if I were a dog, Cooper would be patting me on my head.

"Turn around and let us see what treasure I have brought to Cooper," Drew ordered.

His words reverberated through my brain. I was being talked about as if I were an object?

"Drew..." I couldn't go through with this anymore.

He merely cocked a questioning eyebrow at me. My defiance disintegrated.

Damn. Why couldn't I just say no?

Slowly, I turned and watched them in the mirrored walls as they ogled me. I resisted the urge this time to cover myself. They wouldn't want me to do that. I quelled the momentary rise of disobedience.

"She is a very pretty piece," Cooper said. I relished that tidbit of appraisal. Wanted more compliments. I was disappointed when Cooper dropped his gaze from me and studied the bag of toys on the cart. For some weird reason I wanted both men looking at me again. Despite this horrid situation, I wanted to be their centre of attention. Was this some insane coping mechanism?

"What other toys do we have to play with," Cooper asked as Drew sifted through the bag.

"We've got lube. She enjoys vibrators. This kind," Drew said.

I couldn't see what vibrator he had suggested, because Cooper stood in the way, so I gazed at myself in the mirror. The sight of the toy red lips attached to my nipples made my pussy clench. My face wasn't red anymore, but a pretty pink blush highlighted my cheeks. My eyes were dark and sparkled.

I tensed when I heard the crinkle and rip of plastic. "The toys are all clean. Seal packed. Some haven't been opened. We'll use those on her," Drew said.

"First, a little more foreplay," Cooper answered.

"Foreplay? Is that what you call this?" I gasped. He scowled at me, obviously not liking my outburst.

Copper stepped in front of me and I flinched as he lifted his hand. If he saw my reaction, he didn't say anything. He took my chin between his thumb and forefinger and held firm. My pulse quickened as he lowered his head. His other hand settled upon the curve of my left hip. His palm hot and heavy. His fingers digging into my tender flesh.

I closed my eyes as his lips melted over mine like a scorching personal brand. He kissed me deeply. Kissed me so hard that I felt myself drowning in an explosion of tingles.

I jerked and pushed myself against him. The feel of his erection was rock-hard, promised plenty of pleasure and sucked away any remaining self-control. He dropped his hand off my chin and I reached up and sifted my hands through his silky hair, holding his head still so I could really dive into this delicious kiss.

I barely felt Drew's hand as it smoothed over my bared ass cheeks. Barely felt the lubed tip of a vibrator push against my suddenly clenching sphincter. I knew what Drew was doing. He had a fetish for anal. Enjoyed taking me from behind. But I'd always been ultra-tight back there. Now was no exception. I'd loved when he would prepare me with a lubed vibrator before taking me. But with the pressure pushing into me now, pressing past my muscles, I knew this vibrator must be a size of immense proportions.

A blade of pleasure-pain zipped through my back end and I whimpered. At my protest, Cooper's mouth went frantic. Wild tension zipped through me as his lips slanted harder over mine, quelling any further protest. His tongue was a lusty flame as it pushed boldly into my mouth. He tasted of that minty liquor that I smelled on his breath. It wasn't a mere mint candy as I had pondered. This was intoxicating. Dark and delicious. Just like how he made me feel.

Odd, because he'd been here at the factory all day. Unless he enjoyed a secret drink now and then. I liked the taste. I liked his forcefulness and I envied how easily he removed any decision making from me regarding sex.

A sudden realization slammed into me. My two bosses were pushing me past my boundaries. Forcing me to explore my naughty side. To search the deep secretive side of my wanting a couple of men to have their way with me. All my forbidden fantasies suddenly seemed within the realm of possibility.

What was happening here didn't have to go beyond these walls. There might not be office gossip. There hadn't been any inkling of their sexual prowess circulating around the office, aside from their constant private teasing. They were discreet. That was a good thing. Yes?

It was as if a solid wall had just fallen away from in front of me. I could be free. I could be *me*.

I succumbed to the sudden overwhelming freedom and kissed Cooper back. His answering growl of approval snapped through me like an electrical wire of pleasure. This is what I'd needed. To be pushed out of my comfort zone and to have my inner sexual side awoken.

Sensations lashed through my rear as Drew thrust in the vibrator. The machine stretched my anal muscles and the breathtaking pleasure was addictive. I gasped into Cooper's mouth, made myself relax for Drew, accepting the big intrusion.

Drew began a rhythmic plunging. In and out, the toy lunged, until I was gyrating my hips and dancing on my tiptoes. I brought my hands to Cooper's waist and I kissed him harder. A frantic need to be double-penetrated blossomed deep inside of me. The craving exploded and took over my senses. I slid my hands off Cooper's waist and with trembling fingers, I managed to pop the button on his pants. Then I located the zipper.

I lowered it. The raspy sound was like an aphrodisiac to my senses. I could barely wait to have his cock buried deep inside of me.

Suddenly he cursed. Then he was helping me. In moments, his pants and underwear were gone, and I wrapped my fingers around his immense shaft. His cock was huge, hard and powerful as it jerked between my palms. It was a writhing serpent with a mind of its own. Pulsing with heat and authority, demanding to be used. My pussy creamed and answered the call for penetration.

Somewhere in the back of my mind came a warning that I shouldn't be doing this. I ignored it. It was too late. I wanted pleasure. Needed it.

"This is what I want for you, Carina. For us," Drew said in a guttural voice. His lips brushed a line of fire across my shoulder blades. I moaned as he pressed his scorching erection against my right thigh. The long, heated length was an imprint of assurance against my skin. Drew was going to fuck me, no matter what.

I rubbed my aching clamped nipples against Cooper's chest. Sparks of pleasure-pain had me gasping. Cooper broke the kiss and I followed his gaze downward to look between our bodies. I felt my eyes widen and alarm shot through my dazed senses as I saw his enormous erection.

Oh. Bigger than big.

"Bring us inside of you," Cooper ordered in that deep authoritative voice that made me tremble.

Like a robot, I obeyed. I brought his rigid flesh against my vaginal opening. We both watched as his mushroom-shaped cockhead disappeared into my wet vagina. There was a bite of pain as my muscles protested. I hesitated. Would he be too big?

"Inside," he commanded in a rough voice.

My pussy trembled. Clenched. Demanded. My inner thighs were quivering. My ass was clenching around empty air as suddenly Drew withdrew the vibrator. I wanted to be filled back there. To have that pressure and pain sinking into me again.

I became suspended between my old world of sexual resistance and my new world of sexual submission. I knew I had no choice. They were taking me whether I wanted them to or not. My mind had no say. My body was doing all the talking and it wanted this.

I was unable to protest. Too weak to fight what was happening. I brought his shaft into me. My muscles stretched around him. Fear crept through me. *So big.*

"Good, *cara*," he ground out.

Suddenly he pushed away my hands and then thrust his hips forward. I cried out in surprise as his heavy shaft impaled me. Deep. Destructive.

Erotic sensations flooded me at his quick intrusion.

I gasped as he withdrew.

Cried out again as he bucked and his cock pistoned into me. Pressure-pain turned into pleasure-pain and I mindlessly moved against him. My hands swept around his waist as I fought to stay standing.

My mouth sought his, looking for some form of comfort. His lips melted over mine and I whimpered as he began a hard, passionate thrust of his searing tongue into my mouth. With every buck of his hips, his cock sank deeper and deeper into me. He kept thrusting until my vagina opened up and embraced him fully.

Cooper's pelvic bone rubbed against my clit, creating a wicked friction. My entire body tightened and suddenly I was riding a wild wave of arousal.

Cooper withdrew and I moaned as Drew suddenly plunged his lubed cock into my ass. The iron-hard length of his shaft pushed against sensitive nerve endings and I exploded. Vibrations tore through me and I was engulfed in a kaleidoscope of colors and spasms.

I went mindless. My sanity was gone. I was trapped between two hard bodies. Thrown against one man and then the other man like a rag doll as they stroked and plunged and jerked. My identity vanished amidst an endless surge of sensations. My self became misplaced inside of their pistoning strokes, their grunts and groans and the endless slapping of flesh against flesh.

Their mouths electrified my tender flesh. Their eager hands explored my curves. They brought me out of the pleasure waves and then they tossed me right into another one. I shook so hard, my muscles hurt. Tensions burst and then dissolved throughout me. I keened and sobbed as I drowned over and over inside the maelstrom.

I had no idea how long they took me. Hours it seemed like. Every once in awhile they would stop and allow me some brief minutes to gasp for air. I would stare at my reflection in the mirror. Notice how large my breasts had become. How juicy plump my nipples looked trapped between those toy red lips.

Weird burning aches were on my neck and shoulders too. Discoloured hickies from Drew. My lips were puffy, bruised and tingled from Cooper's kisses.

I'd have just enough time to gather my composure before they started all over on me again. Bringing me back into the lusty world of pleasure. Back into the mindless realm of submission.

They had just finished pleasuring me again. My body was weak and satiated. My mind humming in the after-glow, when a ringing sound burst me from my after-sex haze. For a moment, I realized I had no idea where I was, who I was with, or even what had happened. I just knew I was trembling uncontrollably and two hard bodies were pressed in against me. Two big shafts buried inside me, branding me, holding me captive. I felt so...satisfied.

It wasn't until I heard Drew's coarse voice that everything came crashing in around me. Getting trapped. Getting pushed into being fucked by my two bosses.

"Yeah, we're here," Drew was saying. I opened my eyes and saw our reflections in the mirror. I was the filling of a manwich. My body was trapped between two men. Cooper stared back at me; his nostrils were flaring. His blue eyes were dark and dominating. Drew had somehow reached behind him and retrieved the emergency elevator phone.

He was talking to someone on the other end.

My ears buzzed so loud I couldn't understand what he was saying. But I did understand I was still trapped. Their long hard shafts pulsed deep inside of me.

I whimpered as Drew suddenly withdrew. My ass felt empty. I wanted him buried inside of me again.

I whimpered my disappointment and to my surprise, Cooper dipped his head and smoothed caressing kisses over my lips. His mouth was gentle against mine now. Tender. Caring. His lips sipped at mine, like a hummingbird taking from a delicate flower.

I liked this side of him. A lot.

"Get those clamps off and get dressed. The elevator will be moving within a minute," Drew said coolly. He leaned down and grabbed his clothing.

Cooper cursed softly and slid his shaft out of me.

To my horror, I felt abandoned. Wanted them inside of me again. My legs went weak at losing their support. I reached out and grabbed the handrail.

"No time to catch your breath, sweetheart. Unless you want the elevator man to know what happened in here," Cooper said with a wink.

No! This was too private. I needed to gather my thoughts. Figure out what had just happened!

Cooper swooped up my clothing and deposited them onto the toy cart, then started dressing himself.

On trembling legs, I gasped as I removed first one clamp and then the other. My nipples burned as blood rushed back into them. I managed to get all my clothes on and frantically combed my fingers through my messy hair. Then the elevator began to move. My heart pounded insanely fast against my chest as I stared up at the floor numbers.

I thought this was over. I thought I could just get off the elevator, get the toys to where they were supposed to go, grab my purse from the office and go home. I needed that bubble bath now more than ever. However, Cooper and Drew had other plans.

"We'll meet you at your place. And bring along that bag of toys," Cooper demanded in a deep voice.

Drew was studying me for my reaction. I tried to keep from crumbling. I was a hot mess. I wanted them again, yet what had happened should *not* have happened. I knew it would be scandalous if anyone found out. I didn't know what to do.

So, I nodded jerkily as the elevator doors opened. Cooper pressed the number to take me back to our third-floor offices instead of to where I had been going with the toys.

I watched both men step off the elevator. The doors closed and I sighed heavily.

We'll meet you at your place. Bring the toys.

This was one time I was glad I had a problem saying no.

The End

Taken by Two Cowboys

Jasmine Black

Sierra Allan works hard at her late-father's horse ranch. When her step-brother adds her handy girl services to a private auction to help raise money for the failing ranch, she figures there's no harm...but she's surprised when she's "sold" to two sexy cowboys who demand she submit to their dark desires...

Chapter One

"So this is what you're up to while I'm in the other barn sweating my ass off? Writing those stupid love stories again?" My step-brother snarled from the doorway of the empty stable I'd retreated to in order to write out my naughty fantasies.

I snapped my notebook shut. His comment made me feel dirty and despite the coolness of the barn, heat and embarrassment snapped through me at being caught sitting on a pile of fresh hay with my notebook in hand.

"I've finished everything that you wanted me to do. So I took a break," I answered quickly. I didn't dare look up at him. I'd learned he didn't like to be challenged and he was mellow if he thought I was scared of him. The creep.

I could hear his heavy breathing as he stood there. Could feel his eyes rove over me. I held my breath. I didn't dare move. I was trapped with him blocking my only exit. He knew it and I knew it. I needed to be very careful or I'd end up having to battle my way out. It wouldn't be the first time I'd had to fight him off.

Yeah, sure I could scream for help. The one remaining ranch hand, who hadn't been fired yet because we were running out of money to pay wages, might come running, if he was nearby. But I preferred to keep my problems with Sid to myself, mainly because I was embarrassed in the way he sometimes acted toward me with his groping tendencies. Besides, if I said something to my stepmother, she would side with him as she always did. She'd already said if there were any more complaints about Sid from me, I could just pack up and leave the only home I'd ever known.

"I need to talk to you about something." Sid said. His voice was serious and low. I tensed as he entered the horse stall and to my surprise he overturned an empty feed pail and sat down on it across from me.

He smelled of manure so I knew what he'd been doing in the other barn.

"The ranch is in a bit of financial distress," he muttered as he ran a hand over his dirt-smeared face and then he smoothed back his black bangs.

No shit. I had noticed that for months. Sid had fired three of the four cowboys that had worked at Rocking Horse Ranch for so many years. The hands had been hired by my late father and I had been shocked when Sid had let them go.

"I've decided to do a private auction to try and raise some money to keep the ranch going. Or I'll have to sell off some of the land that we aren't actively using."

Anger flared through me and I saw red.

"But this is Allan land. It's been in my family since my great grandfather started the ranch. You can't sell off a square inch of it!"

He glared at me. I noticed his fists clench. He wanted to hit me at my outburst. Screw him! This land was supposed to be mine in the first place! Not his! But my dad had gotten sucked in by Sid's grifter mother.

Within weeks of meeting her, my dad and Sid's mom had gotten married. Dad had secretly taken out a huge mortgage on the ranch and changed the will so that Sofia would inherit everything. Just a few weeks after returning from their honeymoon, my dad had fallen off a wild Mustang he'd been training. He had landed on his head and broken his neck. He'd died instantly. If I hadn't seen the whole thing myself, I would have suspected Sid and Sofia being behind it.

"The secret auction is where you come in, Sierra. We can save the land if we can auction off your...assets."

What the hell was he saying? I didn't like the nauseating smile on his face. When I had first met him over a year ago I had thought him a nice looking man and a good guy. He'd been polite and quiet. But I'd quickly learned he was sneaky. Several times at night I'd been awoken by some strange noises only to discover Sid lurking in my bedroom, watching me. He was thirty and I was eighteen and I didn't think it was appropriate for him to be in my room, especially without my permission.

"My assets?" I asked in a forced quiet tone. I wondered what he meant.

"Your handy girl services. Your experience with ranch work. We'd auction you off. You'd make more money than here and we could use the bucks to help keep up with the mortgage and keep the ranch."

If dad hadn't taken the money from the mortgage and cleaned out the savings to pay for an extravagant wedding, a two-month long European cruise honeymoon trip and the crazy expensive engagement and wedding rings, and who knows what else he'd done with the money, then everything would have been fine. If Sid's mother would just sell those stupid rings to keep the ranch afloat and stop with her shopaholic inclinations by maxing out the ranch's credit cards, then there would be less of a problem. I wanted to say exactly all those things, but I bit back my words.

Sid would just freak out at my suggestions. I wasn't in the mood in seeing a full-grown man have another temper tantrum about his precious mother who could do no wrong. Working at another ranch for pay sounded like a good idea because I wasn't getting paid here for my work.

These people were seriously stressing me out. I needed a break from them. Reluctantly I gave in.

"Sure. I'm up for it."

He said nothing and I dared a look at him. He was smiling and it wasn't a nice smile because it didn't reach his dark brown eyes. I got an uneasy feeling, but I tried to ignore it.

I tensed as he stood. He looked down at me.

"Great. I always suspected you were smart. You are participating in the private auction is for a good cause. Saving this ranch is of the utmost importance, right?"

I nodded jerkily. That was my main goal in life now. Getting back my ranch before these two idiots lost it forever in a bankruptcy auction.

He left and suddenly I didn't feel like writing anymore. The wood slats of the stall were closing in on me. I felt claustrophobic. I needed to get outside.

I shoved my notebook deep into the mound of straw. I'd sneak out and get it later. Then I hurried out of the stuffy barn. Bright late-afternoon sunshine and a stiff summer wind blew against me. The sweet smell of fresh air wafted into my lungs. I breathed deep and gazed around at the rundown ranch, sadness filling me.

Some of the green shingles on the roof were curling upwards. White paint blistered off the white-plank siding of the house and the wraparound porch. The windmill in the backyard creaked and squealed beneath the gusts. The windmill's gearbox and other parts required oiling and the wind wheel needed a splash of aluminum paint. The only thing that looked well-tended around the ranch was my mom's colorful flower garden at the front of the house. That's because I tended to the white daisies, bright sunflowers and pink cosmos every morning when Sid and Sofia were still asleep.

Never had I seen my parent's ranch as neglected as it appeared now. *It doesn't belong to you, Sierra. It's been stolen. Just walk away. Leave it to those grifters. Start over somewhere else.*

Those words reverberated in my head as I trudged toward the ranch. I wasn't looking forward to going inside. Sofia would be in there sitting around and putting on fake eyelashes, plastering on makeup, or trying on dresses from her latest shopping spree. I don't know what my father saw in that woman. Sofia was lazy and cold. The total opposite of my hard-working caring mom.

My sadness only deepened at the thought of my mother. She'd died over two years ago. One morning she had been her normally cheerful self as she'd cooked dad and I breakfast and then afterwards we'd cheerfully talked as she'd walked me up the dusty lane to meet the school bus. When I came home that afternoon she'd been lying in bed, curled up with stomach pains. Dad had driven her to the hospital the next day where they'd run tests and then done some sort of exploratory surgery. They'd sewn her back up saying she'd been full of cancer. Two weeks later, she was dead.

Damn, I hated thinking about that time. Everything had happened so fast. I've never been the same since then knowing that at any split second some bad shit could happen and my life would once again be changed forever.

"Oh, Sierra!" Sofia called over sweetly to me from the living room sofa where she was painting her toenails black.

Black. Just like my mood.

"I have a lovely dress laid out on my bed for you to wear. But first, come over here so I can put some makeup on your plain face. After you put on the dress, Sid can take your picture for the auction."

A picture? What the hell for? And had she said a dress? I never wore dresses. I was a jeans and T-shirt kind of girl. Always had been.

"What do we need a picture for? I'm only going to be working as a handy girl. Doing the same as I'm doing here." Except I was going to get paid!

"You'll be doing more than that. You need to make a good impression. The better you look, the more money you'll bring in."

Okay, what more was I to be doing? Making dinner? Washing dishes? I didn't ask. I wasn't in the mood to find out what other Cinderella duties I would be getting. All that mattered was getting money.

Sofia shook her head and went back to dabbing her baby toenail. I didn't miss the stupid way her tongue stuck out of her mouth as she concentrated on the task.

I just stood there and watched her. She did amuse me at being outfitted in a fancy orange cocktail type dress with matching orange head band in her bleached blonde shoulder-length hair. Dad really must have checked his brains in the manure pile when he picked up this chick in a bar that one night he'd gone out drinking with a couple of his friends who were just trying to cheer him up.

"Just do as I say, Sierra. Why are you always being so damned difficult?" she snapped after she finished with that last toenail and saw me still standing there watching her. Her bright red lips looked severe as she frowned. She was irritated as always with me and motioned for me to sit on the couch beside her.

I did, just because I knew it was useless to argue with the bitch. She took only minutes to plaster my face with foundation, blush, eye shadow and some hideous black clumpy stuff that she insisted would make my eyelashes look longer. Then she brushed my hair. I tried hard not to cry out as the rough brush ripped through the tangled strands of my windblown brown hair. When she was finished, she held up the mirror and I must admit, I didn't recognize myself.

I must have looked ten years older and...pretty. Huh, I actually looked much better than my plain self. I looked feminine.

"Now go get on that dress so Sid can take a picture. Then after, get supper started. I'm starving," Sofia ordered.

I really should have told her where to stick supper but being the mannerly person I'd been raised to be, I kept quiet.

Besides, she'd already lost her focus on me. She put her feet up on the coffee table and wiggled her newly polished toes so the little fan she had there could dry those precious nails of hers.

In her bedroom, which had once belonged to my mom and dad and now smelled of too much perfume, I found a gorgeous dress laid out on Sofia's frilly white bed.

I had to admit, I really liked the dress. It was an ivory color with a halter-type bodice. When I got out of my clothes and put on the silky garment and then gazed into the full-length mirror that hung on her closet door, I sucked in a breath.

I didn't recognize myself. The dress had a plunging V neckline that accentuated my breasts. The fabric was soft and pleated and left my shoulders and back bare. A fabric belt made my waist look much smaller than in reality. The sapphire-colored eyeshadow brought out the blueness of my eyes.

I twirled around and the skirt part of the dress billowed up just like that dress Marilyn Monroe had worn in a classic movie I had seen on tv with my mom years ago.

"Wow," I whispered.

I was in awe at how I had been transformed. No more tom-boy look. I was a woman. It made me think of my favorite two cowboys, Zane and Zac, who'd worked here. Sid had fired them awhile back because he couldn't pay their wages.

I had noticed how those two had looked at me, especially after my dad had passed. Their hot gazes made me tremble with a fierce need for their touches. What would say seeing me dressed up like this?

Would they have liked me? Would they have taken me away with them? I hadn't seen hide nor hare of either of them since then, but I sure had fantasized about them. Had been writing about them out in the barn in my notebook.

I twirled around again and again and giggled softly. Above my laughter, I heard a weird sound and to my surprise I spied Sid standing in the bedroom doorway. He was taking pictures of me! I stopped and felt really self-conscious as he lowered his camera and leered at me.

"These shots will look great for the auction. You are going to bring in big bucks, Sierra." He smiled that weird smile that didn't reach his eyes, then he quickly turned and left. Suddenly I felt really dirty and I couldn't wait to get out of this pretty dress. Besides, supper had to be made and then evening chores were waiting for me out in the barns.

Would this dreary life of servitude ever end? I shook my head. Some day I would figure out a way to get this ranch back into Allen hands. Some day I would enjoy the shocked look on Sofia and Sid's face when I kicked their lazy asses out of my life and off my ranch. Some day...

Chapter Two

"I still can't believe that someone would pay all that money just for my handy girl services," I told Sid as he drove the pickup truck along the highway.

He just nodded and kept his eyes glued to the road.

The auction had happened within a few days of Sid taking those pictures of me. Two men who'd just inherited a ranch in the next state had bid for a year worth of my services. Some of the money would be paid to Sid upon delivery of myself and then the rest would be paid monthly to me. The deal included room and board.

I was excited to get away from both Sofia and Sid. They'd been unusually happy and their sweetness toward me over the last few days had been nauseating to say the least. Maybe they were glad to see me go. I didn't know why they would be since I did most of the work around Rocking Horse.

Last night I'd signed some papers that stated I would be working for Triple Z Ranch in Wyoming. They had a big spread of a thousand acres, so it should keep me busy. Why I hadn't just told Sid to screw off with his auction and simply fly the coop and find a job on my own, I don't know. Call me stupid. Naive. Or just plain...well, yeah, dumb. I was stupid to be sentimental and want to stay at the home that been stolen from me. A place where I had grown up. A place I wanted back with all my heart.

"The turn off is just up ahead," Sid muttered.

He slowed the truck and we turned onto a dusty dirt road. I noted a brand new looking bright red archway at the entrance that boasted black painted words Triple Z Ranch. We travelled beneath it and kept going for another half an hour. On both sides of the road the land was flat with lush green pastures that were scattered with black horses. Their coats shone beneath the sparkling sun. I could tell the animals were well looked after.

A few minutes later I spied a large sprawling log ranch house. It looked well-kept and homey with a red shingled roof and splashes of red paint on shutters that adorned the abundance of black-framed windows. There were many outbuildings strewn around and all were made with logs and the red color theme.

Wow. No wonder the pay was going to be above par. I suddenly had to admit that Sid's idea of a private auction had been a good one. I would be able to save Rocking Horse Ranch. I just needed to have patience, save my monthly pay and get enough together to make a down payment when the ranch went into foreclosure and it was only a matter of time before that happened. But first I would need to figure out exactly how all that bank stuff worked, because my dad had handled all that stuff and now Sid took care of the mortgage payments so I didn't really have much of a clue.

Sid parked the truck in front of the ranch. We both got out. The August wind was hot and it blew through my light white T-shirt and caressed my warm skin. I caught sight of some of the Grand Teton Mountain Range way off in the distance. The mountains looked pretty, but I would be too busy working here to ever take a trip to see them up close. Sid grabbed my two suitcases from the back of the truck and motioned for me to follow him up the stairs and onto the wraparound veranda.

He knocked and within a few seconds the door swung open. I was surprised to see who stood there. It was one of the cowboys that Sid had fired from Rocking Horse!

"Oh my gosh! Zane! I didn't know you worked here," I cried out. I was so happy to see him that I impulsively threw my arms around his waist and hugged him tight. His body tensed beneath my touch and his heart thumped fast as I pressed my ear against his warm chest.

Wow. This was too good to be true. Zane had always been so nice to me. He'd teased me playfully through the years and I'd had a long crush on him. Still did. I'd hoped that maybe he'd even ask me out sometime. He hadn't. And then he'd been fired.

As I let go of him I caught an odd look flash between Zane and Sid. It unsettled me. I got the feeling maybe Zane wasn't so happy to see me? But then he looked at me, smiled and tilted his head, indicating for us to come inside.

It was cool in here. A welcome relief to the heat outside.

"Nice to see you again, kid," Zane said as he led us into the living room. He walked to a nearby wall and he touched the picture frame of a large portrait of this ranch. To my surprise the picture moved sideways to reveal a wall safe.

Wow. He had access to the ranch safe? I watched as he tapped in some numbers on the number pad and then he opened the heavy-looking metal door. He withdrew a thick envelope, then closed the door to the safe. The painting automatically slid back in place.

Zane strolled over to Sid and handed him the envelope. I couldn't see Zane's face but I did hear an angry gruffness in his voice.

"You can count it outside. Rest assured it is all there. You can go now."

Sid frowned and nodded. Said nothing to me and just left. What an asshole. Not even a thank you. Yep, I was stupid to be doing this. I should be the one with the money packed envelope. Man, why was I such a dunce?

"Thirsty?" Zane asked. He had turned to face me and was gazing at me with an interesting expression in his dark brown eyes. I'd seen him look at me like that before. I'd always felt myself heat up and this time was no different.

"Something really cold, please," I answered. He nodded and told me to follow him. He led me into the kitchen. It was a nice room, decorated in pale green and white. Stainless steel pots and pans were piled here and there. A long oak table took up the middle of the room. There were four chairs.

He reached into the fridge, brought out a beer. Twisted off the top and handed the cold bottle to me. I eagerly drank the frothy liquid and moaned with delight as it slid down my throat. I hadn't realized I was parched and I swear I'd never tasted such a good beer before in my life. Maybe because I hadn't been so thirsty before.

"I get the feeling Sid didn't tell you everything about the deal we made through that online auction." He sounded a bit down, which was weird as I had hoped that he was as glad to see me as I was to see him.

"Well, he said you would pay him a finder's fee of five grand and the rest belonged to me."

Zane shook his head. I liked the way his long scruffy hair bounced with the movement but I didn't like the way he was frowning.

"Yeah, I figured he'd screw you over. Didn't you read what you signed?"

I shrugged my shoulders. I didn't want to tell him that I'd broken my glasses several weeks ago and I didn't have any money to buy a new pair. Sofia and Sid had turned my request for another pair down flat, telling me to go out and get myself a job. Well, I had one now. A good one by what Sid had told me. I'd be helping to tend the horses. Feeding them, grooming them and taking them out for daily rides.

I wondered exactly how dishonest Sid had been with me about what was in that contract.

"Hey! Anyone here!" A man called out from the area in the house where we had just come from.

I inhaled sharply at the familiar voice. Could it be?

"In here!" Zane shouted back.

I held my breath as heavy footsteps stomped into the kitchen.

It was Zac! The other cowboy Sid had fired from Rocking Horse! He was almost as tall as Zane. His hair was shorter and lighter, combed back off his face. He wore dusty cowboy boots, tight black jeans and a dusty looking red and black checkered shirt. His face was well-weathered and tanned.

When he saw me, he shook his head and made a funny animalistic moan that made my nipples tingle and my pussy quiver with awareness. His dark eyes widened and he smiled. I wanted to jump into his arms and tell Zac how grateful I was that they had rescued me from Sid and Sofia but there was something in Zac's smile that warned me he was *more* than just happy to see me.

"Oh great, you're here, baby doll. I need you bad. Some hot and heavy afternoon love is all I've been thinking about since we bought you at that auction. I hope you brought that dress that makes you look so vulnerable and sexy. Put it on will you?"

My tummy hollowed out in a not so good way.

I looked to Zane. He averted my gaze. *Bought me? Vulnerable and sexy?*

Oh no. What exactly had I not read in this so-called agreement?

When I didn't say anything, Zac looked to Zane. Eagerness was quite evident as he rubbed his hands together.

"So how about it? Are we ready for play time? I am aching like a son-of-a-bitch," Zac growled.

How about what? Play time? Aching?

To my shock, my vagina clenched as I began to suspect what was being said. My mouth grew dry. I wished for another ice-cold beer.

"Why don't you grab a shower? She'll be ready in just a few minutes." Zane said.

Zac frowned, then nodded. He left.

"What is going on?" I asked. "What did he mean by afternoon love?" I wasn't sure I wanted to know. I just wanted to leave. I wondered if Sid had gone already. I made a move toward the door, but Zane caught me by my wrist and held tight.

I gasped in surprise as he pulled me against him. I swallowed and trembled at the thick bulge of his erection as he pressed it boldly against my abdomen. He nudged his mouth against my ear.

"Willing women are hard to find around these parts, Sierra," he murmured softly. "When we saw the auction for your ranch, we bought the entire ranch...including your services. Including you, Sierra. Yes, that envelope that I gave Sid contained five grand and it also had a cashier's check for Rocking Horse Ranch. We get your services and you get a great monthly wage. After one year, that contract says you get your ranch back in exchange for a down payment to us on your ranch."

I blinked with shock. I could get my ranch back?

"Consider yourself a mail-order bride, kid. It is all perfectly legal and it is a done deal. So if you know what's good for you, you'll be nice to us, Sierra. We really need a woman. And after a year you are free to go, but I'm pretty sure you'll be sticking around because we aim to pleasure you until you can't walk or see straight."

Oh sweet heavens. I was not hearing what I was hearing. I barely realized he'd let go of me and was now pulling me out of the kitchen and along a back hallway. I could hear the water running in a shower somewhere.

My heart began to race. I tried to bolt. But Zane held me wrist tighter and pulled me toward the last door along the hallway. He stopped in front of that door and gazed down at me.

"That's your room behind this door. You will give us access to you twenty-four seven. Do you want your ranch back?" he asked in a strained voice.

I nodded numbly. I couldn't believe what was happening.

"You can leave right now. I can drive you to the bus station. But you can't go back home, sweetie. The ranch belongs to Zac and me now. There is a clause in the contract that if you decide to leave, you forfeit any claims to Rocking Horse Ranch. After Sid fired us, we got jobs here on this ranch. The owner of was an elderly man. He had no wife, no kids and no kin.

He suddenly died. To our surprise, he left us the ranch and everything else he owned. We're rich now and we already have a property manager on the way to take care of things at your place. The manager will hire new people who will take care of the animals and maintain the property. If you stay here, tend to our needs and submit to our dark desires, the ranch will be back in your hands. That's what was written in the contract. Where are your glasses? Put them on. It will only take a few minutes to read. I don't want you going into this contract blind."

If he was allowing me to read the contract, then it must be true. Excitement like I had never experienced before raced through me. I could get the ranch back. My exhilaration quickly died. I could get the ranch back if I submitted to them.

"What exactly did you want me to do?" I asked. I was scared at what his answer would be.

His gaze softened.

"Everything we want you to do, kiddo."

"What?" I muttered. Was he for real?

"We've wanted to take you for quite some time. But your dad...well he was a good man. He wanted better for you and we didn't want to hurt him. Then he was gone and all the rest of the crap followed. You'll have me and Zac to pleasure. Just the two of us...for now. We'll break you in gently. Just say the word now. Are you in? Or do I give you a ride to the bus station?"

"Zane, I'm...inexperienced." I was feeling hot again at what was running through my mind. Having sex with the two of them? Twenty-four hours seven days a week access? This was not the way I had envisioned my days or nights to be like at the Triple Z Ranch.

"We want inexperienced. We can mold you to our dark ways."

What the hell did he mean by that? I didn't want to ask. Didn't want to know. At least not yet.

I could have Rocking Horse Ranch back in a year. That's all I had ever wanted. I would do anything to get it back. I knew what my answer to Zane and Zac was going to be.

* * * * *

I trembled in confusion as I stood in my new bedroom. I wore that pretty dress that Zac had asked me to wear. Now I understood why Sofia had insisted I pack it. That bitch knew that *I* had been sold off in that auction. I still couldn't believe this was happening.

Zane had been kind enough to give me half an hour to get ready for them. He'd brought my suitcase to my room and before leaving he'd informed me to wear no underwear and no bra and to put on that *special* dress Zac had requested earlier before he'd gone off to shower.

My room was small but nicely decorated in blue hues. The walls and curtains were a light sky blue. The floors were pine-planked. The four-poster mahogany bed was king-sized and took up a good portion of the bedroom. The comforters, sheets and pillowcases were all a dark-sapphire color. I even had my own adjoining bathroom.

It didn't go missing on me that strong steel eyelets had been installed in the shower stall and on the sides of the bedposts. Despite being thrown into this…arrangement so quickly, my mind buzzed with scenarios of bondage. One minute the idea of being restrained while a man or two fucked me, freaked me out. Then the next minute the idea of what was happening, excited me.

Confusion at my whirlwind of feelings was an understatement.

Now as I gazed into the full-length mirror that hung on the back of my open closet door, I didn't even look like me. That tomboy appearance of hastily brushed brown hair, blue-jeans and T-shirt was gone, replaced once again by that curvy woman in a hot-looking dress and fancy face I had briefly seen in my parent's old bedroom.

Earlier, my hands had shaken as I'd brushed my hair, applied the blue eyeshadow, blush and red lipstick Sofia had also insisted I pack. I seriously had not thought I would ever need the makeup on this ranch job. Obviously, Sofia had known what I had unknowingly signed on for.

A soft tap on my door made me stiffen. I licked my dry lips. In the mirror, I spied the door swing inward. Zane and then Zac stepped into my bedroom. Both men wore nothing but black boxer shorts. Bold erections pushed against thin material and I had little trouble making out the long and thick outlines of their cocks.

Heat and fear zipped through me. What had I agreed to? Was I totally mad to be doing this? I was a virgin, saving myself for marriage. I realized that that old-fashioned idea was about to be dashed. How could this be happening to me?

Their harsh breaths shot through the quiet air as they both came up behind me. They looked at me in the mirror. Their heavy-lidded eyes told me the whole story. They wanted me and they were going to have me.

I trembled.

"Have you fantasized about us over the years, Sierra?" Zac suddenly asked. His voice was thick with arousal.

Without thinking, I nodded.

The corners of Zac's mouth tipped upward ever so slightly. He seemed pleased with my answer.

"Did you dream about both of us taking you, kid?" Zane whispered.

They hadn't touched me, but heat whipped off their muscular bodies and pierced my dress to caress my now ultra-sensitive flesh.

"I'm not a kid," I whispered. Not a kid anymore and I purposely did not answer his question about my dreaming about having sex with both of them. I have several notebooks full of hot scenes of both men taking me. In some scenes they took me against my will. Other scenes I willingly allowed myself to be double penetrated. My heart sped into overdrive at thinking about all of those naughty fantasies.

Zac arched a dark eyebrow at my response. He nodded slowly. I whimpered involuntarily as they looked over my shoulders, their hungry gazes dropping to look at my breasts.

I was struggling to breathe now. The dress bodice was suddenly way too snug. Heck, the dress felt like a straight jacket on me. I wanted it off.

As if reading my thoughts, Zane reached for my right shoulder. His palm was like a fiery brand as he touched me. I jumped at his scorching touch.

"Let's get a good look at what we bought," he said. His voice had turned hard and I shivered as wicked tension tore into me.

"Relax," Zac ordered in a dark voice.

I tried. But couldn't unwind. Who could? I was sensing something big happening.

Sexual awareness had me focusing in on their features. Their lips looked luscious. The cords in their necks were thick. Their broad shoulders and wide chests brandished tanned muscles that bulged with their every movement.

I hadn't had a chance to do up the zipper on the back of the dress, so it was easy for Zac to pull the material off my shoulder. He lowered it until my right breast popped free.

Both men inhaled. I made a move to cover myself but Zane reached around and grabbed my wrist, stopping me cold. I caught his reflection in the mirror. He was shaking his head. I didn't protest as he led my hand back to my side.

"Keep your hands down," Zac ordered gruffly.

I nodded jerkily. Tensed again as Zac's hand slid over my other shoulder, hot and heavy. A moment later, my other breast popped free and I struggled out of the sleeves.

"Very pretty," Zane whispered as they both gazed.

My breaths were quickening. My body trembling.

"Turn around," Zac ordered.

I hesitated. Heat fused my face. My cheeks were so hot I swore flames would fly out of them any second. My legs wobbled and I felt faint as I turned around to face them.

Never in my life had a man seen my breasts before. My doctor was a woman so this was both embarrassing and to my shock, quite stimulating too.

"Consider tonight your wedding night," Zane grumbled.

Oh boy.

To my surprise, both men lowered their heads. I cried out and jerked as calloused hands cupped my breasts in vice-like grips. I couldn't escape. Zac parted his full lips and sucked my left nipple into his hot mouth.

Zane quickly followed. I moaned as his hot mouth enveloped my right nipple. Nerve endings sizzled and pleasure burned through me at lightning speed, leaving me gasping at the intensity of their mouths suckling my nipples. I yelped as Zac suddenly nipped on my tender bud, then he licked it, soothing my throbbing flesh.

Something was sizzling deep inside my pussy too. A naughty need was awakening. I wanted to explore it. Instinctively I reached up and speared my fingers through both men's hair and pushed their heads and mouths harder against my breasts.

It was as if the sane part of me suddenly didn't exist and a mindless, unrestrained part of me, was slowly taking over. I tried to reign that uncontrolled part of me in. Tried to think. But their mouths continued to sip and draw, their tongues lapped and licked. Each brush of their rough lips brought more erotic sensations tearing through me. Brought more hot moisture gushing down my vagina and into my panties.

Suddenly a harsh desire to give into an unexpected burst of tumultuous sensations roared through me. I lost it and I exploded. Pleasure crashed into me and I gyrated my body in a stimulating dance. I didn't care what they thought. I sank into the hunger that possessed me. I cried out as waves pummelled me over and over. Then as quickly as it appeared, the intense pleasure vanished leaving me a trembling mess.

The two cowboys continued sucking on my nipples. They were so sensitized now they throbbed with hurt. I wrenched against every lick, gasped at every strong tug and pull. I untangled my fingers from their hair, wanting them to stop.

They didn't. The raspy hair on their faces burned my flesh as they continued nibbling and sucking. I could barely stand now; my legs were so weak from the orgasm. I wondered if they'd even noticed I'd had one.

Both men were groaning. Their fingers kneading the plumpness of my breasts. Their wicked mouths devoured me. They were latched onto me like crazy glue. Would they ever let me go?

I keened my distress. They growled in answer. Their sounds sent blades of tension through me. I began to tremble as another layer of awareness rippled through me. My pussy spasmed. My ass clenched.

Suddenly Zac let go of my nipple. His lips were red as he stood. His gaze was tight with arousal and his eyes glittered with sexual intent.

Zane remained at my breast and I noticed his free hand had slipped into his underwear and he was stroking his cock.

I swallowed at the sight. Whimpered as Zac reached down and slid his fingers into the elastic band of his shorts. He brought the material down over his hips and let his underwear fall down his legs. I cried out as his long, thick and engorged cock popped out at me, uncoiling like a giant serpent.

"Does this live up to those fantasies in your books, baby doll?" Zac murmured. He grabbed the base of his cock with one hand and stroked the immense length with his other hand.

My books? How did they know about my personal stories?

"Sid told us you write in the seclusion of the barns. Sofia said she sneaks peeks at your stories while you are out doing your ranch chores. Said your writing really turns her on. Said you want to know how it feels like to get fucked by two cowboys. Is that right?"

I swallowed at the dryness in my mouth. I didn't know what to say. I was shocked. I thought I had done a good job hiding my notebooks and all this time Sofia had been snooping through them and telling people about my intimate fantasies.

"Yes," I whispered. Humiliation breathed into me. No use hiding the truth.

I yelped as pain zipped through my nipple where Zane nipped and then growled at my breast.

"Get used to the pain, baby doll. It's part of the contract that you signed. We've got plenty of similar treats for you over this coming year," Zac said.

Treats? Is that what they're calling pain these days?

I suddenly wasn't sure I wanted to be on board with a contract I had never read.

Remember your ranch, Sierra. The ranch is top priority.

Renewed defiance raged through me. I *would* handle anything they wanted of me.

Chapter Three

I tensed in awareness as Zane suddenly lifted the skirt part of my dress and slid his hand in between my thighs. Instinctively I widened my legs and a finger swept into my wet vagina. He withdrew his finger and then began a slow massage on my clitoris. Sensations swirled and I moaned involuntarily as my pussy clenched.

"Hmm, I think I want a taste of her, Zane. Let's move her over to the bed before she falls down," Zac ordered in a firm voice.

Oh thank you! My legs were trembling so badly and my head was whirling so much I needed to lay down.

Zane gave out what I figured was a growl of protest. Then he let go of my hurting nipple and moved his head away from me. His eyes were so heavy lidded that it seemed as if he was sleeping. But he grabbed my hand and led me over to the bed.

"Sit on the edge," Zane ordered in a harsh voice. It appeared he was pissed off at being disturbed. I wondered how long he would have stayed at my breast if Zac hadn't interrupted.

I plopped down on the bed, my sore breasts jiggling. Zac didn't waste any time. He reached down, grabbed the hem of my dress and peeled it off of me in one rough swoop, leaving me totally naked. Embarrassment fused heat through me and I barely noticed Zac ball up the dress and then toss it away as I tried to cover my pussy from their view with my hands. Zane's firm shake of his head had me stopping myself.

"Keep them at your sides. No matter what," Zane growled in a stern voice that had me obeying.

In an instant, Zac dropped to his knees, grabbed my knees, widening them. I barely got a chance to see how red and swollen both my nipples were when Zac's head dipped between my shaking thighs.

Wicked pleasure ripped through me as his mouth melted over my pussy. His lips swiftly sucked on my labia creating an instant burning pain as he pulled. Impulsively I reached out and grabbed his head, wanting to push him away.

Zane shook his head at me again, his gaze dark and warning.

"Never touch unless you are told to. Keep your hands away from his head. You are an object now, Sierra. A vessel for our pleasure."

I almost groaned out loud in protest at Zane's words, but Zac's mouth suddenly became gentle and he tenderly lapped my pulsing clit. Pleasure swiftly rained through me. I dropped my hands away, opting to tangle my shaky fingers into the comforters. I held tight as Zac had his way with me down there.

The slurps of his mouth mingled with my whimpers of arousal. I liked the sounds of sex. It was like dark delightful music pulsing through me.

The pleasure he created destroyed my self-control. The muscles in my lower belly quivered. My pussy was on fire. I jerked and twisted as he nibbled and slurped all my sensitive areas.

Suddenly the mattress dipped as Zane sat on the bed beside me. His hand touched my chin. He urged my face sideways so that I would have to look at him.

His mouth was flushed a rosy red from being attached to my nipple. A light sheen of perspiration whispered across his forehead. His feathery hair was in disarray. I gazed down and noticed how long and thick his shaft looked as it angled up toward his taut abdomen.

His cock was big. Scary big. Blue veins crisscrossed his shaft and his mushroom shaped cockhead was flushed an angry purple.

Oh my goodness.

"You look so tasty, Sierra. Your body is so vulnerable and available to us. I don't think we'll ever go out to work again. We'll just stay here and take you over and over," Zane whispered. His cheeks were flushed as he gazed at me.

I could barely hear him. There was a noise in my ears as the heated blood rushed through my arteries.

Zane's arm curled against my breasts like a steel bar and I barely realized he was pushing me backward. Suddenly I was staring up at the ceiling. The upper half of my body was on the mattress while my spread legs dangled off the bed, Zac holding my thighs apart, his head still buried between my legs.

I curled my fingers harder into the comforter and my thighs shook violently as Zac stroked my pussy with his eager and long tongue. My clit throbbed with erotic pleasure and flames of arousal kept my hips jerking.

I wasn't sure how to handle this onslaught of wicked sensations. I could barely form a thought as Zane leaned over me. His head lowered. My mouth came alive with tremors and tingles as his warm lips seared over mine. His hand settled on my left breast and he plumped and kneaded my flesh as he kissed me. He kissed so deeply that I could feel the pleasure arrowing into my mouth down my throat into my body and zinging deep inside my pussy to meet the pleasure Zac was creating.

This was crazy. Crazy good.

My thoughts weren't processing anymore. I was defenceless. I was just feeling. Wrapped inside pleasure and pain and everything in between as my body became theirs to play with. Their naughty mouths made love to me. Rough, calloused hands caressed my flesh urging me toward something I could only perceive as heaven.

I drowned in the tumultuous sensations. Became lost within the pleasure of their touches. Vanished inside the sensual sounds of sex.

I was just gone. I loved it.

I cried out as I was ripped out of my euphoria when Zac suddenly thrust a couple of fingers deep into my pussy. He began a swift pumping motion which quickly pushed me toward an orgasm.

My body grew so tight I hurt. Everything hurt. I needed satisfaction. Needed release. Big time.

Just before I could explode, Zac eased off. Frustration clawed through me.

"Please," I whimpered. I needed them bad. Needed them thrusting into me. Filling me. Fucking me.

Zane stopped the intoxicating kiss. His hot breaths zapped across my face.

"What do you want, baby?" Zane muttered.

"Take me." I moaned. I couldn't stand the need that rushed through me.

Zane ignored me. To my sudden exasperation, he moved his head away and settled his mouth over my right breast. He drew my sore nipple between his firm lips and began a mind-blowing suckling that had me so high-strung I swore my sanity would splinter apart into a million pieces.

Oh man! I was going to die if I didn't get relief.

I twisted against Zane as he continued to suckle. He playfully pinched my other nipple with his fingers. The raspy hair on his face burned my flesh. I could just imagine how parts of me would look red and bruised when these two were finished with me. If they ever finished with me.

I shuddered as I heard the slurp of something. Realized Zac had withdrawn his fingers from me. My eyes had closed and I found it difficult to open them. But I forced myself to and discovered Zac standing nearby at the bedside table.

He was licking his red moist lips and squeezing a tube. Clear gel squirt onto two of his fingers. When he placed the tube onto the nearby dresser, I spied the words *lube*.

Oh geez.

I swallowed as nervousness rushed through me. My ass clenched. I knew what he was up to.

He caught me watching him and he smiled. It was a sexy smile, full of naughty promises.

"You taste like a feast, Sierra. Just as I knew you would," Zac said and then licked his lips again.

My pussy quivered as I remembered the wicked feelings his tongue had created only moments ago.

I whimpered as Zac tapped Zane on his back.

I was ready. More than ready for whatever they were going to do to me. There was no way I could say no to them. Not ever. This pleasure was too good. It was even better than the fantasies I wrote down in my notebooks.

Zane growled that pissed off growl I'd heard earlier. He didn't like being disturbed, but he moved away from my throbbing breasts and then crawled to the middle of the bed and lay down.

Zane looked angry. Muscles in his cheeks twitched and his gaze was full of fire and lust. He was breathing just as hard and fast as I was and his cock jerked as he reached down and ripped open a foil packet to produce a condom.

Have mercy. He really was so big, I thought as I watched Zane sheath himself with protection.

"Climb onto him," Zac ordered, nodding to Zane.

To my surprise, I didn't even hesitate. I was a puppet now and they were pulling my strings. I spasmodically got onto my hands and knees, moved to Zane. He was watching me with those heavy-lidded eyes that really looked sexy.

I was glad I'd been duped into coming here. Glad this was happening. I'd probably think differently after it was over, but right now, I just wanted release.

I climbed over Zane. I made a move to grip his shaft, to bring his hard-looking flesh into me, but he shook his head. His hands came up and he held onto my hips. Tight like a vice.

"Zac will prepare your ass first. Then he'll take you. Then I'll take you."

No! Why are you doing this to me? I need both of you right now!

I wasn't sure if I was begging out loud or if the words were merely reverberating in my splintering mind. But the thoughts stopped the instant Zac's lubed fingers pushed against my ultra-tight sphincter.

I tensed with a jolt of panic as reality came crashing into me.

"I've never..." My words died as Zac pushed his lubed fingers into me. I wanted to remind them I was a virgin, but my thoughts disintegrated as immense pressure seared my ass. I tried to squirm against the intensity as Zac gently moved his fingers against my tight, tense muscles but Zane held tight.

"Easy, baby doll. We know what we're doing. You just accept it and we'll make you hurt really good," Zane said in a hushed tone.

I swore I was going to go mad.

Zac withdrew from me. I whimpered again and again at the sound of lube being squirted over and over as he thrust his fingers into my backside. Every time he entered, he prodded deeper and massaged my anal muscles until they gave way to his prodding.

"Soon, Sierra, soon," Zane soothed.

I inhaled a shuddering breath and nodded jerkily. Finally Zac stopped. The rip of foil split the air. Condom. More slurps of lube followed. I could barely breathe now.

The mattress finally dipped and I looked over my shoulder to spy Zac climb onto the bed. Suddenly I was afraid. For a second I wasn't so sure I wanted this to happen.

I mean, this shouldn't be happening. I'd signed a contract under duress.

But then Zac was in position behind me and Zane tugged on my hips, angling me downward. My hesitation went bye bye as Zac pulled apart my buttocks.

Zac groaned and I gasped as the tip of his condom-sheathed cock nudged past my ring of muscles. I wailed as he pressed into me.

The pressure was immense. The bite of erotic pain intense. The pain quickly faded, and I was seriously stuffed with Zac's shaft.

"Hot and tight," Zac ground out.

I keened as he withdrew and then slid into me again. A little harder this time. Deeper. My ass muscles protested the stretching intrusion and then quickly clenched around him, welcoming him with hugs. Zac moaned, then he withdrew just as quickly as he'd entered, leaving my mind a swirling mess.

I went nuts with frustration as Zane poised his shaft at my vaginal entrance. Then he pushed into me. A violent burst of pain made me cry out in shock. Then the most breathtaking throbbing followed as my vaginal muscles grabbed and convulsed along his hard length.

Instinctively I gyrated my hips melting into the pleasure pain.

Zane brought me down fully onto his shaft until I was gasping from the pressure. Then Zane lifted me off his shaft and Zac speared into my ass.

They quickly fell into the sensual well-coordinated rhythm. Pumping into me so hard and so fast they hurled me toward a swirling vortex.

Each thrust, every piston, tore whimpers out of me as jolts of electricity sizzled through me turning me into a spastic ragdoll. Each plunge of their shafts destroyed my sanity and drove me deeper into the ecstatic pleasure.

Suddenly the two cowboys disintegrated as I became lost inside a mindless kaleidoscope of colors, wild sensations and body-wrenching shudders. Somewhere deep in the back of my mind, a thought popped. It was a beacon that I sensed would eventually lead me back to sanity.

An inner voice warning me that all this exquisite pleasure and pain was going to be well worth it to get my ranch back into my hands. Well worth it, indeed.

Then that thought slipped into the vortex and I was sucked back into the swirling pleasure.

The End

Taken by Two Firefighters

Jasmine Black

Firefighter Kendall Farell has always been attracted to the erotic beauty of the hot flames that dance in burning buildings. Her dangerous fetish could cost her her job if anyone ever finds out. When she's caught flirting with fire and rescued from certain death, her two male co-workers want payback in a very naughty way...

Chapter One

It was hot. So hot I could feel the heat of the apartment fire scalding my bunker gear. It felt as if the skin all over my body was going to start blistering and then ignite at any second. I ignored the discomfort and concentrated on the gorgeous orange flames that danced and writhed like fire-people right there in front of my eyes as I walked back through the smoke-filled rooms after searching for anyone that might still be in this particular apartment. I couldn't locate anyone and my job was effectively done here so I allowed myself the pleasure of submitting to the beauty of the erotic flames.

The colors were magnificent. Amber, orange, ice-blue and virgin white. The colorful flames mesmerized me to the point that I wanted to meld with the inferno.

"Kendall! Get the hell out of there! The ceiling is going to collapse any second!" My partner's gruff shout echoed through my ear mic.

But I didn't want to listen to Kyle Powers. I wanted to study the glowing crimson sparks that were dropping all around me like rain. Grey smoke billowed, curled and breathed, its tendrils like fingers beckoning to me. It was all so damned beautiful.

Watching fire had turned me on for as long as I could remember. The times dad took us camping when I was a teen, I would stare into the campfire. There had been something about the flames that just made me feel as if I were on fire myself. Sexually on fire I mean.

Fiery heat pounded my pussy and my ass as I sucked in a few quickening breaths of oxygen that poured into my mask. My nipples felt as if they were on fire as they pressed boldly against the layers of special fabric that protected me.

"Everyone get the fuck out! Now! The building is going down any minute! Out! Now! Move it out!" Chief Phil Aerius bellowed through the ear mic. I paid him no heed.

He was one of those firefighters who preferred to play it ultra-safe. He was boring.

The roar of the fire as it surrounded me was like music. The tempo thundered through my blood; the pounding rhythm matched my racing pulse. Man, the beat was so erotic.

I began to dance with the fire. Dance like the fire. I moved slowly, seductively, like a flame. I was daring the fire to make love to me.

I wanted to tear off my gear. To be free inside the firestorm that licked at the walls of this building. Above me, the white paint blistered and bubbled, turning the color of burnt umber. Thick black cracks appeared and spread out like tentacles across the ceiling. It kind of reminded me of cracking lake ice or the top layer on spoiled milk. I'd never seen anything quite like this. It was all so beautiful. So artistic.

I blinked at the crazy thoughts. Wow. Was I nuts? Or did I just see things other people couldn't?

A loud rushing sound snapped somewhere above me. I looked up and studied the huge glowing orange lumps that fell from the cracks in the ceiling. The chunks looked like Halloween pumpkins. The burnt black areas looked like eyes and mouths.

I blinked at the scorching sight, hypnotized by the prettiness. It was like I was on a high or something. Like the drugs I'd experimented with in high school. Those drugs were dangerous and I'd quit...but I'd found a greater high by dancing with fire.

Pain broke me from my trance as something hard slammed into my back. Suddenly I was off my feet and in the air.

I hit the floor belly down and hard. Real hard. The wind was knocked out of me. I struggled to catch my breath as something heavy landed on top of me.

Shit! Had the ceiling caved in on me? For a second I wondered if the oxygen tank strapped to my back had been damaged. Oddly enough, I felt no panic. I never freaked out when I was around fire.

"Two down! Need assist!" Kyle's shout rang in my ear.

Damn! Two firefighters down? Where? I needed to get to them. Needed to help them.

Guilt slashed through me. While I'd been dancing and flirting with the fire, two of my comrades had gone down. I had to get out of here! I reached up to pry the heavy thing off my back but it wouldn't budge. I tried harder.

"Dammit! Stop fucking moving! I have a fucking ceiling beam burning into my legs. I saved your ass, sweetheart. If we get out of this one, you fucking owe me. Big time."

It was my partner's voice.

I suddenly realized he was the one on top of me and not the ceiling. That he'd called in help for us. He had taken the ceiling? Wow, impressive. The guy had probably saved my life. My hero.

I could feel the knot of his erection pressing against my ass. Had saving my ass turned him on? Or maybe it wasn't playing hero that had gotten him excited? Maybe the fire electrified him too? The idea of finding someone with the same kink as I had, excited me.

"In your dreams," I mumbled back at him. But I couldn't stop myself from grinding my ass against his growing shaft.

He groaned and then said softly, "Plenty of dreams, sweetheart. Plenty of fantasies of you."

He had fantasies of me? How interesting.

I gasped as the gorgeous orange flames that were dancing in front of my eyes parted. A black silhouette erupted through an open doorway. Water splashed against my visor, snapping me back to full reality. Someone was hosing us down. Disappointment and frustration clawed through me as the flames went away. My partner's heavy body lifted off me.

"Can you stand?" It was Phil. Our chief.

"My, what a big hose you have," I chuckled as I struggled to get up.

"You'll be getting a good look at it soon. You owe me for saving your ass," the Chief growled.

Deja vu. It seemed these guys wanted to get a piece of me. Well, I do not sleep around with my fellow firefighters.

To my surprise I was suddenly finding it hard to breathe. Something burned into my lungs. Smoke. I began to cough. Gagged. My equipment had been damaged!

"Can't breathe," I gasped. I faltered as weakness snapped through me.

I winced as the guys swore. Half a moment later, I felt my mask get ripped off. Hot air burned my skin. Cool air breathed against me as another mask was placed over my face. I sucked in the sweet air as strong arms wrapped around my waist. I had a guy on each side of me, holding me up.

Kyle stumbled and I remembered he'd been injured. I grabbed around his waist and helped him to remain steady.

A moment later, we were following the hose out of the burning apartment unit, stumbling down the smoke-filled stairs, and into the street. As we headed toward a waiting ambulance, I heard the thundering crash as the structure imploded. The pavement beneath my feet trembled as the burning roof of the five-story building collapsed.

Damn! That had been a really close call.

"Hey, how's your legs?" I asked Kyle. He'd been in the burn unit of the hospital a few days now and I'd been visiting him every day after getting off work.

Call it guilt, concern, whatever, I was just glad he was going to be okay. When the ceiling had fallen in, some shards of wood had ripped his pants and burned the back of his legs. They had kept him sedated and so I'd sat quietly and held his hand while he'd slept. Today, he was awake. He even had some red color in his cheeks and when he saw me enter his room, I noticed a bright spark flash in his eyes.

Wow, he was excited to see me?

"I saw you dancing," he said. His softly spoken words made me freeze. I tried to smile, but my face felt frozen.

"What? Dancing? Me? You know I don't dance. It's why I never go to the Firefighter's Ball. You know that better than anyone. I've turned your invitations down for years." Oh geez, I had better shut up. I was sounding nervous.

Kyle smiled. Dimples popped out in the sides of his cheeks. Oh man, he looked so cute when he smiled.

"You can't get away this time. I know your secret, Dancer."

Dancer. Oh great. Now I had a nickname?

His voice took on a cool, serious tone.

"If I hadn't come along when I did, you'd be dead, Dancer."

"So? What? You want a medal?"

"I want you, doll face," he replied.

An interesting chill skittered up my spine.

"Sorry but as you all know, I'm not into firefighters."

There was no way in hell I would *ever* hook up with a freaking firefighter. Both my parents had been in the business. Dad had been caught inside a towering inferno. He hadn't made it out alive. I'd been eighteen. Mom had left the firefighting business shortly after to raise my two younger sisters. But I'd been bitten by the fire bug and began training right out of high school.

"If you want me to keep your little secret, then you'll listen to my proposition."

I rolled my eyes. Man, this guy had nerve. But that was Kyle. He had big balls. Bigger than most. I'd seen him in the change room plenty of times. His shaft was quite the size. Too big for me though.

He had plenty of confidence too. He ran into burning buildings and rescued people under dire circumstances and he came out unscathed.

Except for this time.

I hadn't realized how much I liked him until I'd almost lost him. Emotions, thick and raw and unwelcome bubbled up inside me. I could see now that I had gotten way too close to this guy. Damn! I needed to work on keeping up the walls around my emotions. I didn't want to end up like Mom grieving over a husband and having to support kids with minimum wage jobs just because she didn't have experience in anything else and no time to go back to school to learn something new.

"Sorry, I don't do propositions." I turned to leave, but his next words stopped me cold.

"You'll hear me out or I go to the Chief with your secret. You'll lose your job and they'll declare you incompetent. No more fire dancing for you. You belong to me now; doll face and I will take you any way I can get you."

"You have no proof. So, fuck off," I snapped.

"Fucking you is on my agenda, Kendall. You'll do as I say and you'll do it with that gorgeous smile plastered on your face. And I even have a big fireplace in my bedroom. I'm sure that will come in handy for your fire fetish. Besides, you owe me for saving your life."

Asshole. I needed this job. Needed to keep saving lives and get my regular fire fix or my life wasn't worth living.

I swallowed as he glared at me. He had the sexiest, most dominant look that sent shivers of excitement racing through me. I tried to stem my unexpected arousal at his demands, but it didn't work. I knew in order to save my job I couldn't say no to him.

"I need proof," I whispered.

"You'll get it. When I get out of here, you'll get it."

Reluctantly, I nodded.

Chapter Two

It took Kyle a month before his burns were healed enough for him to return to work. Up until then I'd been avoiding his phone calls. But now with him back on the job, he had me right where he wanted me. To my surprise, he didn't say much on his first day back. All day I was on edge and hoped that maybe by some miracle he would drop his blackmailing idea. At quitting time, when I opened my locker to grab my street clothes in order to change, I inhaled sharply at the twelve-inch long, four-inch-wide red box adorned with a white bow that had been set upon my shoes. My name was scrawled in black pen on the front of the box.

I peeked around to make sure no one was watching, but the locker room was empty.

Hope crashed through me. Maybe Kyle had seen the error of his ways and this was an apology present? Even as I lifted the lid, I sensed it was no such thing. My heart began a mad pace as I spied the three plastic-wrapped red butt plugs nestled in white velvet. Each plug was a different size.

Oh my. Kyle was into anal. I sighed when I spied his handwriting on the inside of the lid.

Kendall,

The little butt plug is way too small. The middle butt plug just won't quite fit. But the big butt plug will fit perfectly for what I intend to do to you. Leave the largest one in.

My place. Next Friday. Seven p.m. Dress nice. No panties. No bra. Check out the evidence. An arrow angled toward the inside of the box.

Anger rippled through me. Evidence. What evidence could someone have of me dancing in a freaking burning building?

I followed the arrow and spied a flash drive tucked into the side.

Crap! He did have proof. Arrogant bastard!

I slapped the lid back and shoved the box into my purse. Quickly I changed into my street clothes.

By the time I got back to my apartment, I was seesawing between fury at being caught on film and inexplicably aroused at being forced to have sex with Kyle.

In the bathroom, I opened the box again and gazed at the smallest plug. Mentally I calculated how many days I would need to wear each plug in order to be ready for next Friday evening.

I'd never worn a plug before. Never had anal done to me either so I was grateful for the instructions inside the container.

But first, I had to find out what evidence Kyle had on me. I slid the flash drive into the computer and within a minute I was watching myself erotically gyrating my hips amidst a firestorm. Snapping yellow flames were lapping up the walls and orange sparks were falling like confetti from the ceiling. I appeared to be oblivious that my life was in imminent danger. Sure, I could argue that the person dancing could be anyone, but my badge number was on my helmet and my name and number were prominent on my protective gear in the fiery light. Flashes of my face appeared behind the safety mask.

I frowned. How had I not seen anyone filming me? Usually I was so careful. I had gone through that apartment. No one had been inside that unit or maybe I hadn't checked as much as I should have because of the beauty of the fire? I'd gotten careless and allowed myself to get caught. I shook my head in disgust. I deserved to be blackmailed.

A little while later, I was outfitted with the plug. The pressure inside my ass was erotic. I liked it. I began liking the idea of having forced sex with Kyle too. Not that I hadn't thought about engaging in some one on one with him before this had happened. I had. Any red-blooded woman would go gaga over Kyle's perfect good looks, his muscle-laced body and that stallion-like cock.

I trembled as fear lanced me. His shaft was ultra-big. Would he fit into me? My pussy quivered at the idea of having him frantically thrusting into me. My ass clenched around the plug as I imaged him sliding his rigid erection into my ass.

My breaths were coming fast and I was toying with the idea of masturbating when the damned phone rang. The intrusion destroyed my imagination and my arousal.

"Hello!" I snapped.

"I know your secret," came a hoarse whisper.

I shook my head. Was this guy for real? What an idiot.

"Stop goofing off, Kyle. I already got your message in the locker room. I saw the evidence. I have the first plug inserted. Just keep your big mouth shut and I'll do whatever you want."

Silence followed. But I could hear someone breathing. It appeared what I had said had turned him on.

What a dick head.

I was about to hang up when his next words stopped me cold.

"I didn't send you any plugs."

What? Was he kidding? I stopped and held my breath. Come to think about it, that voice might not belong to Kyle.

"Kyle?" I whispered. My grip on the receiver tightened. I felt lightheaded. I had made another mistake.

"Sorry, baby. I'm much bigger than Kyle. Go to your door. Open it," the mystery man directed.

Shit. This isn't Kyle? Who the hell is it?

My mouth went dry. Had Kyle told someone about my fire fetish? If so, all bets were off and Kyle could go straight to hell!

Okay, chill. Find out what this guy knows.

"I have no secrets," I blurted.

However, I was pretty sure my quivering voice was giving me away.

"Saw you dancing to the fire. It was beautiful. You are fearless. Let's see how fearless." He sounded aroused.

Immediately I thought back to that night. There had been only Kyle and myself left in the burning unit that night. Unless...

I closed my eyes and inhaled several deep breaths in an effort to calm myself.

"Chief?" I was barely able to hear my own voice so I was surprised that he had heard me.

"Bingo. Now go to your door and get the present I left for you. Don't hang up. Bring the present over to the phone so I can hear."

I swallowed and nodded numbly. I was so screwed. My secret was out. If the Chief decided to tattle on me I would be out of the fire fighting business forever. Devastation urged me to do as he instructed. I placed the phone receiver down onto the coffee table and a moment later, after checking my peephole to make sure no one was on the other side, I unlatched my security chain and opened the door. Right there on the floor was a flame-orange colored box a bit bigger than a shoebox.

Awareness burned through my pussy at the intricate design of fire on the package. Glancing around to make sure no one was watching; I leaned over and grabbed the box and brought it inside. I returned to the phone with the package.

"I have it," I whispered in a breathy tone that surprised me.

He didn't say anything so I began to rip off the wrapping paper. I tried hard to ignore how the living room lights played with the orange flames. A matching colored box emerged, flames and all. I pulled open the lid and inside lay a gorgeous snow globe. But there weren't any sparkling white snow flakes like you'd find in a traditional globe. Instead, there was a small building and as I moved the trinket, my breath caught at the holographic-like orange, blue and yellow flames that leapt from the windows and swirled around the globe.

I couldn't stop myself from staring at the flames. They were gorgeous. The colors of orange burnt umber and gold melded with each other creating a spectacular explosion. They were the same colors that I loved to watch in burning buildings. The flames had to be made from some wild combination of chemicals or chemical reactions. They were so realistic.

I shook the globe and the fire burst higher and danced and swayed and caressed my senses. The familiar arousal swept through me. Wild tremors coursed deep into my vagina and I gasped as my muscles clenched the plug.

"I can tell you like it," the Chief said softly.

"It's...attractive," I admitted.

"It should keep you excited and ready for us."

"Us?"

My heart pounded against my chest. I swore I was going to have a heart attack if I didn't calm down.

"Kyle and myself. At his place. One week. We'll see you there."

Oh-my-gosh!

Two men knew my secret. I was so screwed.

Chapter Three

The week passed by with the Chief and Kyle not mentioning our upcoming meeting. Thankfully, there weren't any major fires like the one I'd lost myself in a dance with that seductive fire. There were the usual small incidents; kitchen grease fires, garbage fires, and grass fires.

However, the fire globe that the Chief had supplied, kept me busy, just like he said it would.

Whenever I played with it, I got hot for sex. By the end of the week, I was both nervous and aroused at the prospect of being taken by two firefighters.

Because of my avoidance of dating a fireman, I'd never had sex with one. Let alone two. So, imagine my surprise at being eager at doing the dirty with two of them, instead of being pissed at being blackmailed. The Chief and Kyle held my career in their hands. I would do whatever they wanted.

Last night I realized I truly had nothing nice to wear. My closet was filled with leisure wear. Nothing fancy. So, I did an online search for nearby shops and discovered a flirty little sex shop a couple of blocks from my apartment. I could have ordered something online, but none of the shops offered same day shipping.

Embarrassed as hell was I as I walked into the shop. Thankfully, a young saleslady put me at easy very quickly. Half an hour later, I had a naughty dress.

Twenty-four hours later I stood in front of Kyle's condominium in a ritzy part of the city. With trembling fingers, I grasped the brass knocker and gave it a few hard knocks. I held my breath and waited. I was quite aware of the large butt plug that filled my ass. It was an ultra-snug fit. Nervousness flooded me. How in the world was I going to accommodate two large shafts?

I jerked as the door suddenly swung open. Kyle stood there. He looked sexy hot. His hair was messed just the way I liked it and he was dressed in a pair of tight black slacks and an unbuttoned white shirt that showed off a mildly hairy chest and bulging muscles.

Kyle emitted a low whistle as his gaze roved over me from head to toe.

"Shit, Dancer. You really clean up well. You are a fox."

"Cut the compliments, Kyle. Let's get this over with." I'd injected an icy crustiness into my words. I didn't want him or the Chief knowing how much I was looking forward to this forced ménage.

Kyle's lips upturned and he stepped aside. He bowed slightly and waved an arm in a signal for me to enter.

"Me casa is your casa," he said.

"In your dreams," I retorted. I entered and he closed the door. He passed by me and led me into a foyer that was decorated in icy blue tones that did nothing to cool the fires of excitement and nervousness coursing through me.

"Your choice, Dancer. Left into the living room so you can mellow with some wine, or up the stairs, to the bedroom and a nice crackling fire in the fireplace."

I didn't want to appear too eager, but I needed to get on with this get together because the curiosity about what was going to happen was killing me.

I headed for the stairs.

"Now you are talking, Dancer," Kyle said. He followed me.

My legs felt weak and wobbly as I ascended. It was a good thing he had a sturdy handrail, because it might keep me from sinking to my knees if I went into an excited faint.

"Second door to your right," he instructed as we reached the second floor.

"Where's the Chief?" I asked as I stopped in front of the open doorway to the bedroom. No one was inside.

"He'll be here. And just so you know. I told him nothing. The bastard had been watching you, just like I had been."

I wasn't sure if I could believe him about the Chief, but what was done was done. As I entered the bedroom I was anxious but also impressed with the decor.

My immediate focus went to the fireplace. My breath quickened. It was set with dark grey brick and a roaring fire crackled in the hearth.

"You like?" Kyle asked as he came up behind me and stood very close. I could feel his body heat blasting against my backside. He smelled of after-shave. It was a delicate scent that I really liked.

I nodded. The flames were pretty and I inhaled at the soft scent of burning wood. The fire was real, not some cheap gas imitation. I gazed around the rest of the room.

The walls were painted dark blue with white accented trim. His bed was brass and the bedding light grey and dark blue. Smart combination.

"You decorate nice," I whispered. My gaze drifted back to the fireplace. I was instantly mesmerized by the lapping yellow flames and the glowing orange embers.

"Hired some professional to do it," he muttered.

I nodded and said nothing.

"Want some wine?" he asked as he strolled to the fireplace. I noticed the black with gold trim ice-bucket set beside the small pile of chopped wood. He withdrew a bottle of white wine from the container and poured some into two of several gold-rimmed wine glasses that had been set on the oak mantel.

He handed a glass to me and I quickly sipped. An ice-cold fruity flavor splashed against my taste buds and I moaned my appreciation.

Kyle stiffened at the sound. He said nothing as he quickly gulped his drink and watched me as I gazed around the bedroom.

I noticed one wall was an entire window with no drapes and I mean no drapes at all. It was dark outside but I could see there was a balcony and plenty of nearby buildings that had windows well lit. I realized anyone could be watching us.

Oh dear.

I took several more swallows to gather courage and soon drained the wine. I was grateful when the buzz kicked in. Alcohol worked fast on me. Always had. It took some of my friends several drinks to get mellow, it took me only a few sips.

"Enough of this shit. I want you," Kyle growled from behind me. His voice sounded dark and dangerous and my heart sped up.

I jumped as the bedroom door slammed shut. Suddenly he snatched away my empty wine glass and to my surprise whipped his and mine into the fire. The glasses shattered as they hit the stone hearth.

Oh my God!

Before I could react, he grabbed my hips and pushed me. I lost my balance and fell onto the bed.

"Son of a bitch!" I yelled at him. I immediately got to my knees and turned to face him. I fought to breathe as he began to undress.

"Hey, just relax. You'll enjoy it. I'm the one in charge, remember?"

Bastard.

He kept his gaze glued to me as he removed his shirt to reveal the bulging muscles in his shoulders and biceps. His pants came off next and I tensed as his fingers slipped beneath his jockey shorts. His prominent erection poked boldly against the material and he pulled his underwear down over his hips releasing the bulging length of his thick shaft. It sprang forth like a giant serpent. His cock looked swollen and bruised, thick and hard. But that's not what grabbed my full attention.

There were flames wrapped around his cock. Orange, crimson and yellow. A tattoo? If I stared hard enough the flames moved as his penis twitched.

I creamed. Hard.

Wow, the guy really was into making sure I got my fire fix.

I was mesmerized by the sight and didn't even realize I was whimpering until he smiled.

"I do love that sound you make, Dancer. I want to hear more."

I barely heard his request as I stared at his blood engorged tattooed shaft. My pussy quivered as he stepped closer and stopped at the edge of the bed. His flame-tattooed cock was mere inches from my face.

"The tattoo is edible, but it will last a long time," he said in a strong, commanding voice.

The air around me grew hot.

"So, eat yourself," I whispered in what I hoped would a defiant tone, but the words came out husky.

Oh damn, I was giving myself away. Impulsively, I licked my lips.

"I have fantasized about this so many times over the years, Dancer." His eyes were sparkling with lust as he stared down at me. He held the base of his huge erection with one hand, and leisurely stroked the nine-inch length with the fingers of his other hand. There was a wild hunger in his tight expression and something wickedly erotic burned through me. It was a heavy intense ache. An almost uncontrollable need for penetration that needed to be doused.

"Suck me. Suck me hard." His hand slid to about halfway up his flame-tattooed shaft as he angled his rigid flesh closer. I could tell by the angry reddish color of it that he needed attention.

He was big. So big. But could he fit into my mouth? Any decision of not doing oral on him was taken away as he gripped my hair and held tight. Then he pushed his thick cockhead against my lips. He smelled like mouth watering citrus fruit and I realized the succulent scent wafted off his tattoo. He moaned in an animalistic way as I opened my mouth.

The head of his shaft pushed in. His powerful rod was hot and stretched my lips. Fear melded with exhilaration as he slowly pressed in. I had to admit he tasted good. Like hot sweet lemonade.

I gulped and struggled to accept his girth. He touched the back of my throat and before I could gag, he pulled back and then pushed in again.

"Come on, baby. Wrap those lovely lips around me. Make love, baby. Make love," he ordered.

I reached up and wrapped my hand over where his hand clasped his shaft. He began a quick thrust and almost immediately my mouth felt erotically bruised.

Instinctively, I hollowed my cheeks, tightened my lips like a vice and began a fast forward and backward bob with my head. His fingers were locked in my hair and with every movement, sparks of erotic pain screeched across my scalp. I liked the pain. It created nice naughty quivers deep inside my vagina.

He groaned louder. Thrust faster and faster. His cock rubbed between my teeth and I slurped the underneath of his shaft.

I teased his pulsing penis with my tongue. He groaned and bucked his hips. I gazed up at his face and watched the pure pleasure wrap around him. His cheeks were flushed red and his eyes were scrunched tight, his mouth slightly open as he gasped for air.

He thrust harder and harder and a few seconds later, his hot semen spurted. I swallowed quickly as he bucked and cried out my name. Not the nickname he had given me. But my real name.

A stupid, giddy happiness exploded inside me. This was an interesting reaction I was having to this forced sex.

When he was finished, he withdrew his flesh, which was surprisingly still hard.

He gazed down at me. His eyes were dark. Darker than I had ever seen them. The look burned a fierce shudder through me. Instinctively, I knew he would never hurt me. At least not on purpose, so my reaction was kind of curious to me.

"Don't get too comfortable, Dancer. That was just the appetizer. More coming." His voice sounded harsh. His warning sent fire rippling through me. My mouth went dry. I wanted him thrusting into me again. Now.

"Not even a thank you?" I teased.

He didn't crack a smile. I got the feeling he was not in a playful mood.

"You'll be the one doing the thanking when we're finished with you," he said in a low guttural voice. I trembled at the harshness underlying his words.

"Are you wearing the plug as instructed?" he asked. He was stroking his cock again. I noticed the harsh redness to his flesh had diminished but his erection appeared to be longer!

" Yes," I answered in a meek voice.

"Good."

Without warning, he stepped forward, reached out and grabbed the front of my dress just above my breasts. One hard yank and the material was in tatters. My breasts bounced free and loose.

Anger raged through me. My new dress was ruined!

"You bastard!"

Impulsively I reached up to slap him, but he grabbed my wrist, stopping me cold. His look was wild. Wow! I liked this untamed side of him.

"You will learn not to wear any clothes in my condo, Dancer. And you'll learn fast. Now, turn around. Show me your ass," he instructed.

He was breathing heavily. My ass and vagina clenched at the sound of his excitement. I was eager to be filled. To be fucked senseless. Lost in hot sex.

Apparently I hesitated too long in showing him my ass, because in a flash he had turned me around right there on the bed. Seconds later, I was on my hands and knees, my ass toward him.

Pleasure raced through me as he lifted my dress. I hadn't worn panties as per his instructions and I felt the warm bedroom air whisper gently against my bare buttocks.

"Such a pretty butt. The Chief is going to enjoy it," Kyle whispered.

For a short while I'd forgotten why I was here, but Kyle's comment about the Chief brought me back to reality.

Damn! I was being blackmailed. I shouldn't be enjoying this so much. But I was so sore. Ached for him. Needed them. Frustration scrambled through me.

"What's taking you so long, Kyle? Why not hurry up and get the Chief up here so I can get on with my night. I have places to go. People to see." I said in a hoarse voice. I was lying. I had nowhere to go. No one to see.

"You will be here all weekend, and every weekend you have off until I say different."

His words hit me like a fiery blast. The entire weekend? Getting fucked by two firemen? I could barely wrap my mind around what he'd said.

"Pretty soon you will beg us to take you," Kyle muttered.

Dream on. But even as I thought about telling him where he could go, I got an inkling he might be right. Especially in the caressing way his hot hands smoothed over my ass cheeks. His touches were arousing. I moaned softly. Blood pounded in my years as one of his hands dipped between my thighs.

Instinctively, I spread my legs wider. Yes, I wanted him touching me there.

"You want to be touched. I can tell," Kyle said. His voice was thick with arousal and my breath halted as his finger touched the opening of my vagina. He dipped his digit inside and before I could squeeze my pussy muscles around him in welcome, he withdrew.

"Not yet, babe," he whispered.

I almost moaned out loud with disappointment.

"Don't move," he ordered.

Awareness rocked me as I heard a drawer open. I dared a look over my shoulder and discovered he had already moved back to the foot of the bed. He was unscrewing the lid from a tube and then lay the tube on the bed near my left foot. Before he could catch me watching, I looked back around and stared at the headrest of the bed.

Earlier, I hadn't noticed certain things, but I was hyper aware now. Eyebolts were all along the post. Delicate chains dangled from some of the eyebolts. On one end of each chain dangled dark brown leather cuffs.

Oh crap!

Kyle was into bondage. Now *that* scared me. I was not into being tied down and at the mercy of two men. I also knew it was useless to protest. He could do what ever he wanted. He knew it and I knew it.

Chapter Four

I bit my bottom lip as I felt my tender ass cheeks being pulled apart. Then came a firm tug on the butt plug. I hissed as he slowly, erotically pulled. My muscles clenched around the toy, not wanting to let it out.

"Yeah, you really like your ass filled. This plug is a bitch to remove. Just relax."

I tried but relaxing just wasn't on my mind at the moment. He pulled harder, and the toy finally left my body. My ass hugged empty air.

Without even realizing it, I wept at the loss.

"Easy," Kyle cooed. "You'll be filled soon enough. It might hurt a bit, but that's what this was for. To ease the pain when the Chief takes you. Once he brands you with his cock, you'll be hooked on anal."

I trembled as a slurp quickly followed. Then he was at my back end again. Slowly, he slipped two fingers against my spinster. My ass, having just been filled by the plug, was eager for penetration.

Kyle moaned as my muscles clenched around his two lubed fingers as he penetrated me.

I shifted my hips as he explored. He withdrew and another slurp followed.

"Three fingers this time. It might hurt. But you will go with the pain. Understand?"

I nodded, eager for him to be done.

My thighs quivered as he pressed into me. A pinch of pain was followed by intense pressure that left me gasping for air. I could hear his breathing was getting louder and faster. Could hear my moans drift throughout the room.

"Take me inside," he hissed.

I obeyed and clenched my muscles around the intrusion. I gasped at the pressure he created and at the heat deep inside. I winced as he cursed.

"Tight. So damned unbelievably tight. You are a virgin back here, aren't you."

I nodded numbly.

"The Chief won't go easy on you. He never does. He will be rocking on you like an out-of-control stallion."

A stallion. Oh no!

I cried out as Kyle withdrew. Held my breath as he slurped more lube.

So much lube!

"Four fingers incoming," he warned. A chuckle laced his voice.

Asshole. This was not the time to be joking.

"How would you like all those fingers up your ass?" I asked between clenched teeth as he pushed into my aching, quivering hole.

"Dancer, I have had a whole hand up my ass a lot of times and I enjoyed it," came his horse reply.

I yelped as his four fingers pressed against my tender muscles.

"How's my mare? Nicely in heat. Ready to be fucked?"

I tensed at the deep rumble of the Chief's voice as it roared through the bedroom.

I hadn't heard him enter. My face heated. Embarrassment flooded me at my boss finding me in this compromising position.

"I'll take over now, Kyle," the Chief said in a commanding voice.

"She's a virgin back there," Kyle warned.

I detected sympathy in Kyle's voice. Expected tenderness from the Chief, but it appeared that bit of news didn't faze him.

" I won't go easy on her then. That would just spoil my mare. I want her to know who is boss."

Despite the shock at his words, I creamed. Hard.

"Nice position. Perfect," he said softly. I imagined the Chief peering between my thighs and to my surprise my pussy clenched. It felt so heavy and pulsed with cream.

I tensed as the mattress moved as the Chief climbed onto the bed behind me. Gasped as the Chief's hands slid against my hips. He held me firm. I tried to struggle. But his force was iron hard. Before I knew what was happening, he was pressing his rigid, unlubed shaft into my ass.

He groaned in a sound that was animalistic. I moaned impulsively as pressure slammed into me.

I almost fell over as he withdrew and then pushed into me again.

I cried out at the painful pressure. He withdrew and let go of my hips. I wanted to bolt away and it took every ounce of my self-control to stay there on the bed.

"Too damned tight aren't you, baby? I'll take care of that. Lube my clock, Kyle."

Kyle was going to lube the Chief? Wow.

I looked back and watched Kyle step forward. The Chief was on his knees behind me and Kyle was lathering lotion all over his rigid erection. I felt a little disappointment that his penis wasn't tattooed too.

But my eyes widened at the Chief's size. I had seen him naked in the unisex locker room at work many times before or after a shower, but he had never been erect like this. Hung like a stallion was an understatement.

Panic at his size slammed through me. The guy was going to tear me apart. Keeping my secret wasn't worth getting injured. Time to go. I made a move to get off the bed, but the Chief caught me by the hips.

"You ain't going anywhere, sweetheart," he warned. My breath halted as he plunged deep in one thrust. Pleasure and pain snapped through me. My thoughts short circuited. My body became paralyzed for the briefest seconds as he impaled me.

"Good girl. Now just hold still. Don't fight me and everything will work out fine," the Chief growled. His words barely registered.

The pressure inside my ass was intense. I exhaled as he withdrew and inhaled sharply as he slid into me again.

My inner muscle gripped him like a glove. He emitted a curse. His hold on me tightened. I held my breath as he began a fast-pistoning motion that shot painful pleasure through me. He fucked me forcefully, his pelvis crashing against my ass as he slammed harder and harder. Faster and faster.

The penetration made my pussy ache for attention. I could feel an orgasm approaching, but I just couldn't grab it. I couldn't gyrate beneath his vice-like hold. I tried to move my hips. Tried to get the motion. But it just didn't work.

Desperation had me clutch the comforter beneath me. I held tight as his rigid flesh plunged in and out.

I sensed if I came. When I came. It would be something so explosive I just might lose my mind.

He kept rocking into me. I couldn't believe how long he went. Sweat blistered over me.

Pleasure and pain had me gasping. I craved having Kyle's cock in my mouth. I heard myself calling his name. It was a desperate wail. I needed my mouth to be filled.

Must have told him what I wanted, what I needed, because suddenly he was right there on the bed in front of me. I accepted his shaft as his hot flesh filled my mouth. I sucked on his rigid cock. Slurped his swollen head. His scented penis jerked and twitched between my lips. It was a powerful serpent and I controlled his pleasure with my mouth. I began a fast bob, wanting to bring pleasure to Kyle.

Kyle groaned.

The Chief moaned.

I whimpered beneath the onslaught of sensations that suddenly took hold. It was happening!

I came apart like one of those fiery industrial explosions that I hose down while at work. I heard the Chief cry out. Felt his cock twitch and pulse inside me as he released himself. He let go of my hips yet continued fucking me.

But I was free now. I was dancing to the fire that shattered by senses. I could see the flames in my mind. A roaring combustion that curled around me like a firestorm. The orgasm was painful as it ripped me apart.

I shuddered and moaned. Cried out and sobbed as the flames made love to me.

Suddenly the chief was withdrawing! So was Kyle! I felt empty. Dead. No!

"No, no, no. I need you." I wailed to both of them. The need for the ultimate satisfaction was like an uncontrollable fever. I was a wreck. My orgasm was collapsing.

How could they do this to me? How could they leave me here like a sobbing hysteric? My brain was fragmenting at the loss of their powerful pistons. A shriek ripped through my mind at their cruelty. This was bad. I was going to lose it.

"Easy, Dancer. It'll be even better when *we* allow you to release," Kyle spoke in a non concerned tone.

I cried. Maybe I was even screaming. I don't know. But the next thing I knew the rest of my dress was ripped off me and they were forcing me to lie down on the bed, belly up. A pillow was thrust under my ass. A tinkle off chains followed.

My wrists were cuffed. My arms were stretched tight. But they left my legs free. If I could only bring them together...

My pussy was sopping wet and achy. I tried to clench my thighs to keep this awesome orgasm going but the Chief climbed onto the bed. His body was tanned, laced with muscles. His balls were huge and his erection was much longer than Kyle's cock.

He had had that monster inside me? I couldn't take my eyes off him. Amazing that I could take something so big.

He moved between my thighs. His wide shoulders nudged against my shuddering flesh preventing me from closing my legs.

Wow. The Chief surely did look handsome. His dark hair was messy. Fire danced in his dark blue eyes. He had a smile. A determined gaze that told me he wanted me.

My body was so tense, it hurt. Man, did I ever hurt. But in a really good way.

"You are seriously wet, baby," the Chief whispered. "Wet enough to put out the biggest of fires."

I was mesmerized at the sensual curve of his luscious mouth as his head descended.

"I've wanted to taste you from the first time I interviewed you," the Chief muttered from between my legs.

"I hope that's not why I got the job?" I mumbled in a hoarse voice.

"One of the reasons," he admitted.

He stared at my pussy and I creamed some more.

"And you being a good firefighter helped. You kept your fire dancing a damn good secret, Kendall. You sure did look pretty though, while you danced with all those flames threatening to consume you. Acting like you didn't give a shit in the world that you were moments away from death."

I tensed as Kyle came and climbed onto the bed. He settled beside me. He didn't look at me as he moved his head over my left breast. I gasped as he palmed my breasts, then he began a slow erotic suckle on my nipple. Pleasure burned through me. His hot lips pulled and twisted, his sharp teeth nipped and scraped.

I cried out as the Chief's tongue stroked between my labia and lapped up my ultra-sensitive clit. I could feel my vagina drop open for him and I just creamed like crazy.

The men were stoking a magnificent fire inside me with their bold tongues. A fire that I sensed would never be fully put out with mere masturbating. The Chief's tongue circled my clit in slow torturous movements that sent shivers of pleasure cascading through me. I clenched my thighs against his rock-hard shoulders. I creamed and creamed as he slurped and he drank.

He sucked so much out of me I was sure I would go dry. But I didn't. His mouth feasted upon my sex. The blistering slurps were noisy. My body heated with perspiration, yet they kept licking and sucking until I just couldn't think straight.

I lost myself within their eager mouths. My breaths became ragged, my body jerking uncontrollably as the two made love to me.

Damn them! Didn't they realize they were driving me insane? My arms screamed with erotic agony as I kept pulling against the restraints. My nipple burned as Kyle sucked. My pussy was on fire as the Chief licked and loved.

I shuddered uncontrollably. I needed release! Needed them!

By the time they freed me from the restraints, I was seriously keening. I caught sight of the Chief lying nearby on the bed. He was rolling on a condom. His cock was purple and swollen. I needed him buried deep inside my ass again. I scrambled to my hands and knees, totally distraught. Totally needing to be fucked.

Kyle was the closest, so I moved on him. I was desperate. On fire. The flames of arousal were burning me alive.

Blackmail or no blackmail, I needed some heavy duty fucking. I grabbed Kyle's shoulders, held him as I pressed my lips over his. He kissed me back. Hard. He thrust his tongue past my lips and I opened to him.

Kyle's hands settled on my waist and I could feel him lifting me. Then I could feel the Chief's wide flared cockhead and then his entire penis slide into my quivering ass.

"Lay back," Kyle instructed. He helped me as I lay down fully on top of the Chief whose hands eagerly swept over my breasts. I hissed as he began pulling and yanking on my sensitive nipples. Then Kyle was coming over me. His engorged shaft protruded like a thick pole.

I cried out as he pressed into my vaginal opening. I reached up and dug my fingers into his shoulder muscles. His nostrils flared as he sank into me.

I gasped at the burning stretch of his throbbing shaft. He was bigger than I had ever imagined. So much bigger.

As he thrust, his rock-hard erection pushed against sensitive nerve endings, sparking pleasure and pain.

"Kyle!" I cried out as I squirmed and adjusted to his massive invasion.

"Dance for us, Kendall. Dance for us, now," the Chief ordered in a choked voice.

Dance? I was stuffed beyond comprehension! Impaled on two shafts. How could I dance?

The Chief stayed inside me; his shaft buried to the hilt. Kyle withdrew and began a quick pistoning motion.

I gyrated my hips, danced as best I could with two poles searing into me. Inside my mind, bright flames consumed me. I moaned and shuddered as lust and pleasure intertwined.

Kyle's fast movements created a maelstrom of sensations. Muscles contracted all over my body. Convulsions snapped through me like lightning bolts and I exploded into a mass of unrelenting convulsions.

My mind climaxed. I saw flames. They were so wild. They encircled me. Held me tight. Hugged me. Burned me alive.

I flew into the pleasure. My screams of release shattered through the room. The squeak of bed springs joined my screams. Both men hissed and groaned as they filled me to perfection.

"You belong to us now, baby." Kyle's voice echoed in my ears as I gasped and shuddered.

More flames ignited. The fire drifted higher, claiming my vision. Orange. Blue. Purple. Yellow. Other colors I could not put a name to.

The flames. They were unlike anything I had ever seen. I jerked and convulsed and danced upon their convulsing erections.

Had I gone mad?

Maybe.

One thing I knew for sure. I was being taken by two firefighters and the pleasure was so much better than any fire I'd ever danced with.

Much better indeed.

Yes! Yes! Yes!

The End

Taken by Two Personal Trainers

Jasmine Black

When dancer Chelsea White discovers her lucrative job is in jeopardy, she hires an extreme team to whip her back into physical shape. But her two personal trainers aren't going to give her just any regular gym exercises...

Chapter One

"Excuse me?" I gasped.

"You heard me, Chelsea. You need to get back into shape or you'll get fired. I heard the boss talking to her boss about you. Said you aren't living up to your end of the contract."

I stared at Ann in stunned disbelief. I had just finished my shift. My feet and my breasts were sore from all that pole dancing and I'd been changing into my street clothes in the employee's locker room, when Ann, a janitor with the hotel had come in with her bucket and mop to clean. When she'd seen me, she'd rushed straight over to tell me the devastating news.

My tummy hollowed out in a really bad way. I earned my living as a stripper at a cocktail lounge in an elegant twenty-story hotel set smack dab in the middle of Los Angeles, California and yeah, I admit I do make a pretty decent living. I work from midnight until six, dancing around a pole in several daring topless costumes. I sleep all morning and almost every afternoon I enjoy shopping with the movie stars in the snazzy shops along Rodeo Drive over in Beverly Hills.

Having Ann tell me that my career was in trouble because I'm not in tiptop shape was a sobering thought. I had to admit, I had let myself go. I'd given up my daily jogs by the beach, swimming in the ocean and surfing. I'd even started to dabble in drinking the free cocktails we got at work.

"Suggestions?" I asked as we headed toward the employee elevator that would take us down to the basement garage where we kept our cars.

"Extreme personal trainers. They are expensive but I heard through the grapevine a couple of our co-workers have tried them and they say this method works. These particular men train you in an unorthodox way and guarantee toned muscles and rapid weight loss."

"Explain unorthodox," I said as I punched the down button and we waited for the elevator to arrive.

"Personal training to lose weight through sex, working out, and a high fat low carb diet" Ann whispered, gazing around to make sure no one was listening.

Yeah, right. She had to be kidding me.

"Seriously, I'm not in the mood for jokes, Ann. You just told me my job is in jeopardy. I need something that works fast. I can't get fired." I loved my lifestyle here too much. There was no way I was going to return to Small Town, USA where everyone knew everyone's business.

"Remember Carrie?" she asked as we stepped into the dimly lit mirrored elevator.

I nodded. Carrie was relatively new here. She worked the late afternoon to late evening shift. I usually came on my shift when she was leaving. But I had noticed a transformation lately and she really looked hot with her toned, tanned muscles and new blonde bob cut.

"She lost twenty pounds in a month. She called that unique personal training company and they sent her two of these big guys who whipped her into shape in no time flat. She said they made her sweat and pushed her past physical boundaries until she thought she would go mad." Ann's voice then lowered. "Chelsea, I think she's trying to get your job. I heard her inquiring to the boss about the midnight spot Friday nights. The boss said she would think about it."

Fuck! No way! That spot was mine!

I had worked my ass off for years to get the coveted times with huge tips and now some new upstart chick wanted to weasel her way into my good fortune? Fuck that shit.

"I need the phone number for this physical trainer place," I hissed.

Ann's eyes widened with shock.

"You're kidding me, right? You did hear me when I said sex with these trainers, didn't you?"

I gulped. Maybe I could work around the sex thing and get them to train me in other ways.

Desperation zipped through me as I caught my reflection in the elevator mirrors. Yeah, I was starting to look a bit shabby and flabby. Damn! Why had I not noticed my appearance was not up to par with the physical clause in the contract I'd signed? I even had a zit on my chin!

Hell, I was not going to lose my job. I was not going to lose my gorgeous beach apartment that overlooked the ocean and if I had to have a personal trainer who pushed me beyond boundaries then so be it.

"Okay, I'll text their phone number over to you as soon as I get home."

"Thanks," I said as we both stepped off the elevator. We waved to each other and parted. As I walked briskly toward my brand-new baby blue Mustang convertible, I spied Carrie getting out of her beat up old black truck. She didn't see me as I slipped behind a post and watched her pass by.

Yeah, she looked great. All tanned and wearing some sexy white outfit with short skirt that showed off sleek feminine leg muscles. What I wouldn't do to get nice legs like that.

God, she looked gorgeous as she walked with a cute wiggle. She had confidence oozing out of her ass. I giggled at that thought and when she disappeared into the elevator, I slipped over to my car.

Yeah, I wanted to block Carrie from getting my position. Heck, who was I kidding? I wanted to be Carrie!

When I got home and checked my cell, Ann had already texted me the phone number. I called and the receptionist who answered was friendly. She asked me a bunch of questions about my job, my goals and if I had any health issues. Then she went into some detail about how hard I was expected to work to get results. There was no mention of this sex stuff Ann had mentioned so I figured Carrie had just been bullshitting about the trainers.

I was pretty satisfied that this place would help me so I didn't flinch at how much money they charged. A few minutes after I hung up, I had a questionnaire and consent form in my email inbox.

I answered the questions, gave my consent, sent it all back and then headed off to bed. I was tired from working all night and I was eager to get some heavy-duty sleep.

I slept a solid eight hours, which for me was unusual. After making myself a cup of coffee, I moved my laptop out onto my balcony and sat at the tiny table I had out there. While I sipped my black coffee, I closed my eyes and inhaled the salty ocean air. I loved the hot July sunshine that caressed my face. Enjoyed the crush of waves that rolled onto the private beach I shared with the other five occupants of this apartment building.

I'd come a long way from that poor skinny kid who lived in a trailer park with her drunk dad. I'd had to scrounge around the garbage cans behind restaurants for scraps of food when he went on a drinking binge and forgot to come home for days on end. Sometimes I'd been forced to beg for money with a hat while I played my harmonica to the crush of tourists who came to our scenic Florida beaches. I wasn't going back to that kind of life.

I shook my head, opened my eyes, and checked my email. A message from the Dream Training Team caught my attention.

As I read the message, my heart picked up a mad pace. They had accepted me into their program and wanted to start training in their gym this afternoon. I looked at my watch. I had less than an hour to get ready.

Oh man! No shopping today. That sucked.

Chapter Two

"Remove all your clothing, keep on your shoes and socks. You can hang your clothes on the hook over there and lie down on the weight bench. Your trainers will be with you in a moment."

My mouth dropped open in shock at what the woman who'd just shown me into this private gym had said. She didn't seem to notice my reaction as she quickly turned and left the room.

Had I just heard right? Remove all my clothes? Would that little tidbit of information not have been in the contract? Oh hell, I'd barely read it last night. I'd merely done a quick skim through and just signed. When I got back home, I had better do some more reading through it so there wouldn't be any more surprises.

My heart pounded like a bitch against my chest as I gazed around.

The room looked like a typical gym. All the walls were mirrored. There were matts scattered about on the floor, weights on shelves, press benches as well as the standard apparatus; treadmill, stationary bike, rowing machine, and plenty of other equipment.

I spied a large official looking poster on a nearby wall. The word RULES jumped out at the top. I hurried over to look. Shock shook me as I read. Sure enough, there were several rules and one of them required the client to be nude at all times while in this area.

This was crazy!

I continued to read.

My weight would be checked daily. If no weight loss occurred within 2 days, I was out on my ass. No refund. I did remember reading that in the contract.

My breath caught at the next rule.

Sex was required as it burned off a lot of fat. The physical trainers were guaranteed to be free of any STD's and they would use condoms. Sex was mandatory every day and at the discretion of the instructors.

Oh my gosh, so Carrie hadn't been lying when she'd bragged about having sex with her trainers.

Shit. Nude.

Man, I really shouldn't be so self conscious about it, I chastised myself. I was a topless pole dancer and I did remove my panties in front of plenty of people. However, I had never had sex with a stranger. This was all happening so fast I couldn't wrap my head around it.

I read through the rest of the rules and by the time I returned to the bench, I couldn't even remember what I had just read. Except the part about being nude and having sex.

My mouth grew dry as I slipped off my running shoes. My hands shook as I removed my blouse and then my shorts. I blew out a tense breath as I ditched my bra and panties. I hung everything up on one of the hooks and then I quickly slid my shoes back on.

This felt so weird being naked with so many mirrors around. Everywhere I looked I saw me with my freshly blow-dried mid-back length straight black hair, my puzzled brown eyes and not so in shape body. But despite having a bit more weight on than usual, I had to admit, I still looked good.

As I lay down on my back upon the padded bench, anger burst through me.

What a bitch. The boss should be kissing my curvy ass with all the money it brought into the club. Instead, she was trying to kick my lucrative butt out the door.

I swore softly, lifted my feet onto the bench, held my legs tightly closed, clasped my hands over my breasts and waited.

It didn't take more than a minute before I heard some men talking. Then the door to my room opened and two big guys walked inside.

My eyes widened when I saw them. And I meant big.

They were loaded with muscles. Hell, even their muscles had muscles. They were tanned with broad shoulders. Strong looking legs.

Very tall. And aside from wearing fanny packs, they were completely naked.

Did I mention big? Like in extremely well-hung.

I grew warm and resisted the urge to fan my face.

The guy on the left, was a bit shorter than the other one. His shaft was a good eight inches long, and his girth maybe two inches or more. He had a plum shaped cockhead and tons of blue veins weaving along the entire length.

The other guy carried a clipboard, but I barely saw it. Instead, my gaze lowered. His cock was even bigger than the other fellow. He was probably a good nine or ten inches in length and fully erect. He had a large mushroom shaped cockhead and a good three-inch girth.

Wow. These guys were going to spoil me with those heavy looking shafts.

I swallowed as both men suddenly fell silent and strolled over to my bench.

"Chelsea White?" The man who carried the clipboard asked. They appeared very comfortable with their nakedness. I wish I could say the same. Man, I'd never felt so...exposed before.

I nodded, completely aware of how their gazes studied my every inch. I couldn't help but notice how good looking both men were too. They had brown hair, dark five o'clock shadows, blue eyes and smiling lips.

Perhaps they were trying to put me at ease with their easy-going smiles? Or maybe they were excited to get in on some sex? I creamed at the thought of getting it on with one of these guys.

"Good, we always make sure we have the right lady before we begin. My name is Hal and this here is Ed," the guy with the clipboard said.

"Hi," Ed said. I nodded greeting to them and noticed that Ed was very busy admiring my nipple rings.

"Let's get down to business." Hal said. I jumped as he slapped his clipboard onto a nearby table and then came back to stand at the foot of my bench. My legs were together and he didn't even ask permission to touch me as he slid his hands between my knees and pulled them apart.

He gazed between my legs at my pussy. To my horror, my pussy muscles clenched in anticipation as he gawked.

"You're nude down here. Good. I like a woman with no hair. Makes for a closer contact. I stay down here longer and you get harder orgasms and stronger thighs. I assume being nude comes with the territory of being a stripper," he said thoughtfully.

My mind reeled at what he was saying. Closer contact? Stay down here longer? Harder orgasms? What in the world?

He let go of my thighs, reached out, grabbed a small padded cushion off a nearby shelf, then placed it at the foot of my bench. I gasped in surprise as he got down on his knees.

My tummy clenched as his hands slid beneath my ass and he pulled me right to the edge of the bench. Then he grabbed my ankles and brought my legs up until the backs of my knees were settled upon his wide shoulders.

"Feel free to dig in with your heels as hard as you want. I don't break easy." His dark blue eyes stared back at me. He didn't smile, but his voice was a soft seductive whisper.

Oh my! This was a unique position I'd never been in before. He then slipped his hands between my thighs and his fingers pushed apart my labia.

I trembled as he let out a low whistle of what I perceived as appreciation. I was so stunned I don't think it was even registering in my mind at what was happening. I felt oddly composed, as if it was suddenly perfectly normal to have two strange men inspecting my intimates.

"Already creaming. That's good. But I'll just get things a tad wetter."

He looked over at Ed.

"You know what to do. Make sure she's tied down."

What? Tied down? Holy shit! What have I gotten myself into?

Chapter Three

I watched Ed as he reached under the bench on my right side and brought up a black strap with a plastic buckle on one end. As he held the strap, he walked to my other side, reached down, and lifted another strap.

I trembled as both fear and excitement pummelled me.

"You'll have to put your arms to your sides," Ed instructed.

Like a mindless zombie, I did as he asked. To protest was to lose all my money. Besides, defiance was blossoming inside me. If Carrie could do this, then I could too. That bitch was not going to take the job I loved!

Ed placed the straps just beneath my breasts and snapped it snug. Then he grabbed a small pad, placed it on the floor on my left side and he dropped to his knees there.

I jerked as he reached out and cupped my breasts. His hands were hot and firm.

"Easy, this is all part of the program" he whispered. His blue eyes twinkled with arousal and he licked his red lips as he descended his head.

My pussy clenched and flowered open as Ed's mouth melted over my left nipple. He sucked firmly and my flesh immediately hardened with pleasure. I shuddered as his teeth compressed on the gold nipple ring and he pulled it until sweet pleasure pain burst through me. He began massaging my breasts, his fingers kneading and plumping.

My breaths quickened and I grew heady.

I gasped as Hal's hot breath caressed my pussy. His hands pushed my thighs wider and his warm shoulder muscles bulged beneath my thighs with his every movement. I moaned and dug my heels into his back as his mouth melted over my clit. I cried out as his lips sucked and tugged on my labia.

Ed let go of my breasts and lifted his head.

"How's that for your introduction to our extreme way of doing things?" Ed asked.

I nodded jerkily. I couldn't even speak. Especially with the naughty things Hal was doing with his mouth between my thighs. He was now licking my clit and my thighs quaked from the pleasure.

Ed chuckled.

"What we are doing is our daily warm up for your muscles," he explained.

Daily? My head spun.

Then he began tweaking my nipples. Pinching and twisting. Pulling on the rings until violent pleasure raced through my tender buds.

Wow, this was some awesome warm up!

Ed dipped his head again and latched onto my right nipple. His lips enveloped my tender flesh and I watched as my nipple disappeared into his mouth. His facial bristles rubbed my skin, creating a sparkling friction that had me gasping.

Between my thighs Hal began to eat me. He was lapping so hard; pleasure screamed through me. I could feel his tongue enter me, then leave and slurp around my pulsing clit. Then in he came again, his long, strong tongue like a miniature thrusting cock.

I creamed over and over and he slurped, thrust, and licked. My vaginal muscles clenched and quivered around the intrusion.

My body tightened beneath their touches, their licks, and their arousing slurps.

I clenched my hands. My hips bucked as tremors roared through me. My feet pressed harder into Hal's back.

My breathing was rough. My moans filled the air. My head thrashed back and forth. I was keening now. I was on fire. I needed release. Needed it bad.

And then I exploded!

I jerked with every lick of their tongues. Convulsed beneath the hot brands of their mouths. I wanted to scream. To cry out as I bucked and jerked and writhed within the spasms. All my muscles clenched and released. They tightened and loosened. Over and over my muscles worked until sweat blistered over my skin and heat drowned me.

They kept me orgasming so long that I could hardly stand the pleasure and pain that swirled around me. By the time they allowed me to catch my breath, I was panting. But I felt exhilarated.

Hal lifted my limp legs off his shoulders and I could barely keep my feet on the bench where he placed them.

"Stay and rest for a minute," Ed said. He unlatched the restraints.

The men stood, then strolled over to a table near the window. I hadn't even noticed all the bottles of water that were sitting there. The men popped open the lids and drank.

My mouth was dry as I lay on the bench and gazed down at my body. My nipples were red from Ed's mouth and my pussy felt hot and throbbed from the endless orgasm.

I gazed at my reflection in one of the many mirrors. My brown hair was tangled and my bangs were wet with perspiration. My eyes were glazed and my mouth was slightly open as I panted.

Gosh! I looked like I'd just been mouth fucked by two men!

"Here," Ed whispered. I turned and discovered a bottle of water being thrust in front of my face.

"Let me help you sit. Just get up nice and slow, so you don't get dizzy. Intense workouts have a tendency of making our clients lightheaded," Hal said. He came to my left side, grabbed my arm and helped me into a seated position.

Yep, I felt a tad lightheaded, but the swooniness quickly went away. I grabbed the bottle of water, twisted off the lid and drank.

The cold liquid satiated my thirst. I swear it was the best water I had ever tasted. After I drank about half, I rubbed the cold bottle against my forehead. The chilly contact felt really good upon my hot, sweaty flesh.

"With the information you have supplied about your work schedule, I've made a physical training schedule to coincide with yours," Hal said as he sat down beside me with his clipboard. He slipped off a sheet of paper and I studied the computerized print out.

My eyes widened as I read.

Workouts during my work breaks? What exactly did that mean? I wasn't sure I wanted to know. I would ask them later. Right now I needed to catch my breath. I was sitting here naked, with two nude men acting as casual as if we were fully dressed.

But my gaze could not help but to wander to each of their erect cocks. How were these men going to get relief if they mouth fucked clients all day long? Wasn't it painful to be aroused without relief?

"Okay if you have any questions about the schedule, give Cindy a call. Right now, we need to get onto the next phase," Hal said.

"Lie on your stomach upon the bench," Ed instructed.

I longed to drink the rest of my water, but I figured it was best to do as they asked.

When I was belly down on the bench, I twisted my head so I could see the two men in the mirror. Ed was at a nearby cabinet. He opened the door, withdrew what looked like a tube and some other item I couldn't get a good look at. But I sure did get a good look at Ed's shaft. It stuck straight out. It was thick and swollen and jerked every so often.

"You will wear what we're about to insert for a few days. It will be uncomfortable, but the discomfort will pay off," Hal said from right beside me.

Wear what? Discomfort?

Oh, I wished I had read that contract before signing it. If I dared ask questions now, they would know and maybe deem the contract null and void. I didn't want that.

I watched Hal in the mirror as he was joined by Ed.

My eyes widened and my tummy clenched with nervousness as I spied Ed squirt some thick lotion from the tube into Hal's palm.

Then Ed was spurting lotion all over a white plastic item. I could see it quite clearly now. One end was tapered and round and the other end was wide with a base.

Oh my gosh! A butt plug. They were going to outfit me with a butt plug? Now I understood. One of these men was eventually going to take me up my ass!

Chapter Four

I whimpered as I watched both men bend over me. My tender ass cheeks were pulled apart and Hal dipped a lubed finger against my sphincter. Gently, he pushed past my clenched muscles and slowly lubricated. I gasped at the intense pressure and moaned softly as my anal muscles spasmed around the intrusion. Both men remained silent. But the slurps of lube shot through the air as Ed continued to spurt more and more onto Ed's fingers. By the time Ed was finished, he'd massaged and lubed the inside of my ass with three of his fingers.

And I was a mess. I wanted his fingers back inside of me. Heck, I wanted a cock thrusting into my ass.

"The instructions on how to clean and re-insert the plug will be given to you by Cindy when you leave," Hal said.

Who wants to leave? I want to stay. I was enjoying his touches.

In the mirror, I watched as Hal moved aside and Ed stepped closer to me. He held up the generously lubed butt plug.

"This will pinch, but just for a minute until the muscles get accustomed to the invasion," Ed said. Then he was lowering the plug, aiming for my ass.

I whimpered as I observed in the mirror. Watched the plug disappear between my cheeks. Moaned as the pressure pushed past the tight ring of muscles and then the tapered end slid in. So far into me I didn't even realize I had such a deep area inside of my behind. The pressure blossomed as the fatter end of the plug entered.

"Just breath deeply and push out your muscles and it will insert easier," Hal said softly from beside Ed. I did as he said.

Both men watched my ass and I noticed their shafts grow even longer and thicker as they observed the plug disappear inside of me. The sight turned them on.

Sweat blistered across my body. I was starting to feel quite warm as the plug went deeper. Then it stopped. The fullness kind of freaked me out. I wasn't sure if I liked this pressure or if I hated it.

Whatever. It was staying. I was in this extreme training for the long haul.

"Okay, it's done. Good job. Now get dressed and let's get over to the weights. We've got a two-hour workout ahead of us."

Two hours! All I want to do is sit here and have them fuck me. How weird is that?

They helped me to sit and allowed me to drink the rest of the water, before allowing me to dress. But they remained deliciously naked! Talk about eye candy while working out.

And so, it went. The rest of the two hours had me sweating my ass off. I pushed weights with my arms, pulled weights with my legs. Rode the stationary bike. Jogged around the gym and skipped rope. I drank so much water that I swear I floated out of that gym. I felt invigorated from all that sweating; however I was truly disappointed that there was no more sex that day.

When I left, I already looked forward to tomorrow.

Upon getting home, I was too bushed to read the contract. Too tired to even formulate any questions as to what other extreme sexual training I might encounter over the next month. I took my first afternoon nap in years, ate a healthy meal at the strip club; salad and steak. Free meals and drinks for employees was another reason I loved my job.

Then I worked. I writhed topless and gyrated my hips throughout the night. For fifteen minutes, I was a cowgirl who whipped around her lasso. Another fifteen minutes I was a topless Catholic school girl with a very short skirt which allowed the patrons to see my bare bum. I wondered if anyone saw the white base of the plug?

Yet for another time slot, I became a vampire with fake fangs and fake blood dribbling down my chin. Despite the aches and pains that nagged most parts of my body compliments of the workout, I felt wild and free for the first time in a long time. When I did my final stint of the night; a balloon routine, where I or certain patrons that I selected from the audience, popped balloons pasted to my body to leave me fully naked, I was exhausted. To my surprise, my tip glass was overflowing with money.

"Wow! What put the sparkles into your steps out there on the stage?" Ann gushed as she met me in the locker room. "I couldn't take my eyes off you every time I passed by. I haven't seen you move like that since you first started."

"I joined," I confessed as I slipped my tank top over my sore breasts. I gasped at the friction my top caused my sensitive nipples.

"You what?" Ann gasped. She looked horrified and then envious.

I nodded, feeling pretty proud. I slipped on my shorts, socks and shoes.

"Did they...have sex with you?" Ann whispered. She gazed around making sure no one was listening. But the two other women in the room; a waitress and a bartender, stood at the far end chatting and weren't paying attention.

"They mouth fucked me. Warm up they said. Then they gave me a good workout with weights and other stuff. Listen, I really wish I could tell you more, but I am so tired. I really need to go home and get some sleep."

Ann nodded jerkily. I could tell she was disappointed that I wouldn't elaborate. But hey, I just wanted to rest up. Usually we walked out together, but this time I just waved and said goodbye.

When I entered the elevator, my eyelids were drooping and I think I might even have slept for the minute it took to reach the employee garage. When I stepped out of the elevator and the cool garage air blasted my face, I was thankful. It woke me up enough so I could drive safely home.

The rest of the week followed the same routine. After work, I went home and slept like the dead. Then I had a healthy brunch, popped over to the gym for a nice mouth fuck by Ed and Hal, followed by getting weighed, which thankfully, I was losing weight. Then came my intense workouts, then an afternoon nap followed by a healthy dinner and then work again.

At the end of the week I noticed my boss was watching my shows with a smile on her face. She seemed impressed with the changes starting in me. My tip jars were overflowing to the point, they had to give me two jars for each show! And the new girl, Carrie, gave me the dirtiest looks!

I was admiring the changes to my body. My muscles seemed toned. There was less flab. I was smiling all the time and I was starting to feel alive again. When the butt plug was removed by the men almost a week later, I wanted it back inside me again. Hell, I wanted a cock inside me. But I didn't get one. At least not at the gym...

It was Friday night and I was enjoying my midnight topless skit. It was my most popular show at the most popular time. I pretended to be a nurse. I wore a white nurse cap with a red cross blazoned across the front of it. I was dressed in a tight, very short white skirt with no undies, knee high white socks and white shoes.

I danced topless, jiggling my breasts at the patrons and giving them glimpses of my bare ass. I touched myself with medical instruments. Allowed forceps to hang off my nipples or my labia for several minutes at a time while the customers cheered. I pressed the stethoscope over one breast and then the other while I danced with my pole.

Then I suddenly spied Hal and Ed out in the audience. I fumbled. *Shit! What were they doing here?*

After the shock of seeing them wore off, I quickly got back into my routine where I stuck a large twelve-inch long with three-inch girth imitation thermometer into my pussy and gave the patrons a good look by lifting up my skirt. My mind jerked as to why my two personal trainers were here tonight. To see the show?

Suddenly I remembered the first day at the gym. They had given me a schedule and I had quickly glanced at it. Something about workouts during my breaks had caught me eye. I'd been so exhausted after that first day at the gym that I hadn't given the schedule, or the contract for that matter, a second thought. I think the schedule was still in my purse somewhere.

When I finished my routine, quickly picked up all the items I'd used for the show and then stepped off the stage, Ed and Hal met me. I waved away the bouncer who was intent on keeping the two men away from me as he thought I was going to be harassed. I quickly ushered Ed and Hal backstage and down the long hallway to my change room.

"What are you guys doing here?" I gasped as I dropped my items onto the makeup table. My cheeks were warm with embarrassment at having them here at my workplace. I had a fifteen-minute break before I needed to get into my next costume.

"Did you not read your schedule?" Ed said with a cool smile. But in the heavy-lidded way he was looking at me, and with that big bulge tenting his pants, I just knew why they were here.

Workout sex. It had to be.

Chapter Five

"Oh, is it tonight that it starts? I hadn't realized how fast time flies," I mumbled as I watched both men lower their zippers.

"Why else would we remove your plug this morning?" Hal replied.

Truth be told, I'd thought maybe they'd give my ass a bit of a break. Let it rest from the plug as the item had been pretty damned big.

I blew out a very tense breath. Work-out sex? Here? At my place of employment? Like, seriously?

"I trust we won't be interrupted for the next fifteen minutes?" Hal asked. He stepped to the door and flipped on the lock.

I shook my head. I couldn't guarantee anything but I didn't dare tell them or they might leave. I did not move as they removed their pants and their underwear. I was paralyzed with fear at getting caught having sex at work and yet I was also bursting with anticipation as their swollen cocks sprang free.

Over the past week, I had grown used to them being naked around me while I'd worked out at the gym. I'd watched their stiff cocks bob or jerk as they leisurely assisted me in my weight training or timed my skipping rope regiment or counted my laps while I jogged around the gym.

During the workouts, I'd drooled over those big, strong shafts. Had begun to anticipate having their engorged flesh impaling me. Had even dreamt about it happening and now the time had come for it to be reality.

Ed removed his shirt and slipped off his shoes. He sat down on my dressing chair and waved his hand for me to come to him.

My breath hitched. I wasn't wearing any undies, just my short nurse skirt. I had peeled off my socks and shoes during my routine, so I didn't have to remove anything.

I creamed as I walked over to him.

"Stand here right in front of me," Ed ordered.

I did what he told me to do. Where else was I going to go? I peered over my shoulder and noted that Hal stood right in front of the only escape route out of here and he gazed back at me with a menacing, "I dare you to run" stare that snapped defiance into me. He was stroking his big cock and there were gorgeous muscles bulging up and down his very big arms. Whether I wanted to or not, I was going to go all the way with this extreme physical training and I meant that literally.

I returned my attention to Ed who was gazing around. He didn't comment, but I got the feeling he might be thinking the same thing as I was in how could we have a genuine workout here in my change room, which was no bigger than an eight-foot by eight-foot prison cell. It was a room that appeared smaller because of all my stuff jammed into it.

Against one wall I had all the costumes hung on hangers. Boxes filled with costume props lined another wall and the rest of the place was cluttered with my makeup dresser, a couple of chairs and full-length mirrors. There was barely enough room for the three of us to be standing here, let alone having sex.

The distinct rip of plastic echoed through the room behind me. I gazed at the nearby mirror and watched as Hal sheathed his big erection with a condom. Then came the slurps of lube.

I trembled.

Ed grabbed my hands and pulled me even closer to him. His fingers intertwined with mine. He gazed up at me with those gorgeous blue eyes. He looked just as sexy as the first time I'd seen him walking into the gym with Hal. Had that been only a week ago?

"The next three weeks are going to be intense," Ed said.

Intense? Like it wasn't already? I resisted the urge to fan my face. I was getting so warm, it was breathtaking.

Excitement raced through me as Ed leaned forward and while holding my hands, he slipped off the chair and got down onto his knees. Instinctively I spread my legs. His mouth easily found my pussy and I gasped and jerked as he began lapping and licking my ultra-sensitive clit. He pleasured me with his mouth until I was bucking against his head and hot moisture seeped down my tunnel and into his mouth.

I struggled to breath as something hot and smooth nudged against my sphincter. Hal's hands slipped over my waist and he held tight. His mouth smoothed over the base of my neck where he rained seductive heated kisses upon my flesh.

Fire lanced through me as Ed's mouth pushed harder against my pussy. My thighs quivered as Hal's shaft slowly penetrated my ass. The pressure of his cock was intense and I gasped as Ed's long tongue dipped into my vagina. I couldn't help but squirm at the double impalement.

I was breathing hard and fast. My tummy was clenching. My thighs trembling.

I began a soft wail. I couldn't stop myself. It just came out of me.

"Shh," Hal warned from behind me. He sucked on an area at the side of my neck until it burned. Somewhere deep in the back of my mind, I wondered if my skin might bruise. How would I explain a bruise to my employers?

The five o'clock shadow on Ed's face sparked a friction burn all around my pussy making me so aware of what was happening. I was being taken by two personal trainers. Men, who were still strangers to me. And I was loving this.

I moaned as Hal withdrew and then plunged his hard cock deep into my ass. My muscles clenched around him, welcoming him. The pressure was exquisite as it burned through me.

Suddenly Ed lifted his head from my steaming pussy.

"You taste good. Really good," he whispered.

Then he was standing and I noticed my wetness around his red lips. He moved closer to me and I don't know how he suddenly had a condom package, but he was ripping plastic and then quickly sheathed himself. He leaned closer and brushed his chest against my sensitive nipples with feather like brushes.

I moaned at the desire he created.

Hal withdrew his penis from my clenching ass and Ed positioned his large cockhead at the opening of my vagina. Without warning, he impaled me in one solid thrust that had me crying out in shock as pleasure exploded through me.

"Shh," Hal said again. As Ed withdrew, Hal pistoned into me.

I tried not to moan, but I couldn't help it. Pleasure waves exploded through me like a tsunami. I was lost inside shuddering waves of arousal as the men drove their swollen cocks in and out of me.

I heard myself keening. Hal shushed me again, but I couldn't stop making noises as pleasure rushed over my senses. Ed's mouth fused over mine, sucking in my cries. His tongue thrust into my mouth like a miniature cock. The impact of having all my orifices filled was body-shattering. Mind-splintering.

Pleasure zinged here and there, awakening intimate centres I never even knew existed. I writhed between their bodies as they pummelled me with their erections. Sweat broke out all over me as they thrust and plunged and brought me to orgasm over and over.

Their strokes were hard and fast, perfectly timed. I was heady as I danced between them like an impaled ragged doll. My muscles clenched, tensed. Every fibre of my being was being worked out.

I arched and bucked against their hard, muscular bodies. They fucked me hard and they fucked me good.

The workout went on for like ever. The orgasms were so deep and so intense that I swore I was pushed into another realm of existence. An intense plane where only the strongest and fittest survived the pleasure and the stamina. Suddenly I knew I would be able to keep my job. I would take this extreme fitness training as far as it would go. I was exhilarated at the idea of doing this every night. I orgasmed yet again. My body shuddering at the release.

Lust pummelled me as their shafts quivered and jerked inside me. Warmth filled me as they came. When they finally slowed, I swear I would have fallen had they not been holding me up with their cocks buried deep inside.

"Your schedule says your next break is at two o'clock a.m.," Hal breathed heavily against my ear as he slowly withdrew his shaft.

"Your next workout is at one minute after two o'clock," Ed said in a strangled voice after he broke his kiss and pulled out.

"Make sure you tell the bouncers that we're welcome," Hal said.

I held onto my makeup table, feeling totally wiped out as sweat poured off me. I blinked away the perspiration as it dripped into my eyes.

The men unsheathed, dropped their condoms into the wastebasket and got dressed.

"Don't be late," Hal winked as he unlocked the door.

And then they were gone.

My pussy ached. My ass felt empty, wept for another impalement. My lips tingled and I could barely think as I tried to remember what my next routine was supposed to be. As I gazed into the mirror, I noticed a big bruise beginning to form on my neck. Hal had given me a hickie. I would have to cover it with makeup. And fast.

My hands trembled as pleasure continued to whisper through me and I began to gather up the clothing and props for my next routine. I gazed at the clock. Sure enough, it was exactly fifteen minutes later. It had been a hell of a fifteen-minute workout and I wondered how many calories had been burned off.

As the after-sex exhaustion wore off I suddenly realized I couldn't wait until my next break. Couldn't wait until I was once again taken by my two personal trainers.

The End

Taken by Two Carpenters

Jasmine Black

A gift certificate from her three besties has Colleen Rue ordering an extravagant pleasure machine from The Sexy Wooden Toy Shoppe, but she quickly discovers that the two well-muscled carpenters have much more in mind than just showing her how their machine works...

Chapter One

"A gift certificate?" I asked my three besties as I stared down at the fancy sheet of gold paper laden with red hearts and black calligraphy writing. I was kind of embarrassed and excited that my best friends had insisted on a get-together at a fancy restaurant for what they called my "first-month anniversary breakup with Bob party". I had been with the guy for three tumultuous years and I'd finally given him the boot.

"It's not just any gift certificate, sweet pea. This one is for The Sexy Wooden Toy Shoppe. The owners are discreet and they're two of the hunkiest carpenters you'll ever meet. Believe me, they make the best adult toys for single women and you'll be all set and not need a man before you know it," Ami said in her calm, smoky voice as she fingered the gold-rimmed wine flute that was half-filled with sparkling pink champagne.

I frowned.

"Isn't this the place where you bought all those wooden toys for your dungeon, Ami? And where Grace's husband bought his rocking horse?" Grace had confessed to them a while back about her hubby's rocking horse fetish.

"That's the one," Ami replied. "And don't forget Wilma's husband got her that assortment of wooden butt plugs."

"They work really well too," Wilma said with a chuckle. "The smoothest plugs I've ever worn."

"Didn't I tell you they would be smooth, pun intended, of course," Ami answered with a laugh. Her green eyes sparkled with excitement and there was a smile on her bright red lips as she winked at Wilma.

Ami was a submissive who enjoyed purchasing toys for the dungeon she shared with her husband and his friends. Just last month she'd had her hair straightened, dyed black, and cut to shoulder length with long bangs because her husband was suddenly into geisha girls.

"But you know I'm not into that kind of kinky stuff. Bob wanted me to do those weird things with him and that's why I finally got rid of him," I said.

Even as I spoke to the girls, I realized I sounded like a prude. I was out of touch with reality. Guys didn't want a vanilla sex partner. Men wanted adventurous and sexually confident girls like Ami, Wilma, and Grace.

"We know you aren't into that kind of stuff, Colleen," Grace said softly. "These two carpenters will make anything your little heart desires. Private stuff just for your own use. No one, including us, has to know what you got. And like Ami said, the guys are discreet. You fill out an order, they build it, personally bring it over and set it up for you and show you exactly how everything works, and I mean everything if that's what you decide."

Grace winked.

Her wink and the way she said "everything" piqued my interest. I was about to ask her what she meant when the waitress suddenly interrupted by asking if we wanted more drinks and if we wanted to order now. Of course, we all did.

I ordered more champagne along with a large Caesar salad and garlic bread on the side. As the others ordered their drinks and food, my gaze flew to the gift they'd given to me.

Hmm, I liked that no one would have to know what I would order. I did have one little thing I wouldn't mind having. Something to help alleviate my stress and to fill my lonely nights while I worked on my erotica short stories. My mind was already whirling with the details.

"Yeah, keep reading," Wilma pointed to the small print area with one of her long black-nail polished fingernails.

I did as Wilma asked and realized the expiry date of the gift certificate was in a month. Near the bottom of the paper was a website url that I could visit to check out their catalog or order something custom-made.

"Ladies, you really didn't have to do this," I gushed after I finished reading.

The certificate was worth two thousand dollars. This was mind-blowing, but it was just like my friends to do something so extravagant. They had money. They were rich. Ami had inherited from a single multi-millionaire aunt and Wilma and Grace had married into rich.

My cheeks felt really warm and I reached for my champagne. I held up the flute and the girls followed suit.

"Cheers and thank you so much. Your generosity and your thoughtfulness really warm my heart," I said. And I meant it.

The four of us clinked our flutes together and drank. Then the conversation turned to Wilma who confessed that she was sleeping with their gardener. I wasn't shocked, because Wilma and her husband, Jim, who was a world-renowned neurosurgeon, had an open marriage.

I leaned back in my chair and watched my friends as they giggled freely and showed off their latest jewelry.

We'd known each other since kindergarten. We all came from different backgrounds and religions and yet we'd all gotten along since that first day we'd met on the playground on the first day of school. We all looked so different, but we were as close as sisters.

Grace, with her beautiful flawless dark brown skin, luscious curly black hair, and a love for animals had become a veterinarian. She had met and married a famously rich racehorse owner.

Wilma, our blonde Barbie doll lookalike, who'd become a nurse, had snagged the doctor she'd always wanted. And Ami, the natural red-haired of the girl clan, who changed her hair color like once a month, was the most adventurous of us, had ended up as a real estate tycoon and was on husband number three who was a real-estate billionaire.

And then there was single me. Mousy brown hair, no husband, no boyfriend and the poorest of all of us girls. I lived and worked in my small two-bedroom apartment where I wrote erotica for a living. It allowed me to live out my sexual fantasies and fetishes safely between the pages of the books I wrote. No way was I going to do in real life what I wrote about nor was I going to end up with a rich hubby like my besties or become a billionaire author.

Ah well, as long as my girlfriends were happy, I was happy. And tonight, by giving me this present, they were very happy. While they continued to chat and drink and eat, I discreetly picked up the gift certificate, folded it and placed it into my purse. An inner happiness burst inside of me because I wouldn't need a boyfriend or a husband to keep me satisfied. What I planned on ordering would replace a man, and I was perfectly fine with that.

"Where would you like this setup, ma'am?" The tallest of the two men whom I had just allowed into my apartment asked as he walked into my hallway carrying some large slabs of wood. He was followed by another man who carried a very large toolbox.

Both men looked just as cute and as sexy as their pictures on their website. They were smiling at me in an interesting kind of way that made my cheeks warm despite the coolness in my apartment thanks to a faulty thermostat that the stupid landlord still hadn't fixed despite it being late November and freezing outside.

These two men knew what I had ordered. They were the hunky carpenters who owned The Sexy Wooden Toy Shoppe. I should be more embarrassed having them know all the intimate details of the item I ordered. Shouldn't I? But I had managed to keep myself relatively calm knowing that after they set up my new machine, I would never have to see them again. Besides, their website said they were discreet and if they wanted to stay in business they had to live up to their word.

"The extra bedroom, please, Thomas," I instructed and led them to the room across the hall from my bedroom.

The owners were attractive. I had to admit. Polite too. I guess they had to be in their line of work.

We'd been in touch through several emails and now they were here. They didn't talk much over the next little while as they came and went from my apartment. They took several trips, returning with more toolboxes and more slabs of pre-cut wood and even some stacks of cardboard boxes. Then they let me know that they would be done in about an hour and kicked me out of the room, so they could work.

So, I left them alone, settled myself with my laptop in my kitchen at my tiny table for two to write. But who could work when one had two sinfully hot looking men setting up a pleasure machine in one's apartment?

Good Lord! What had I been thinking ordering a sex machine?

Stop overthinking it, Colleen! These guys do this for a living! Nothing to be embarrassed about!

My mind whirled with thoughts about what I would be doing every night with that contraption. Or perhaps I should be thinking about what that machine would be doing to me?

Boy, oh, boy. I would have to figure out how to keep the sex machine covered and hidden for when I had guests. Being an introvert, it was rare that I had anyone over. But with my luck, someone unexpected, like my parents or nosey brother, would show up and then my secret might be found. So far, I'd come up with maybe having it securely covered and the excuse, if needed, that I was storing furniture for a friend.

I finally managed to start back to writing, and to my surprise time flew fast. The next thing I knew Thomas was looking over my shoulder and reading my work.

I quickly shut the laptop lid and he chuckled as he leaned close and whispered into my ear.

"Hey, it's nothing I haven't done before," he said.

Good heavens! How embarrassing. He'd read part of a very hot ménage scene about two men seducing a woman in her apartment.

"You write good. Is ménage a secret fantasy of yours?" he asked.

I swear my cheeks had never felt so hot in my life! I struggled to find something to say but came up with nothing. But that was me, I sucked at this kind of conversation.

I did notice he smelled nice. Like pine and sawdust and just a hint of cologne. The scent tickled my senses and I swear if I knew this guy just a bit better, I would turn my head and plant a hot kiss on those luscious looking lips of his.

Man, he even had the faintest five o'clock shadow on his chin and cheeks. It made him look so sexy seductive.

Grab him and kiss him, just for the hell of it! An inner voice teased me. You know that's what Wilma, Ami or Grace would do. They weren't shy girls. If they saw some hottie they wanted, they would go after him.

Good heavens, I could never kiss a strange man, no matter how good looking, I admonished myself.

Suddenly he straightened, and disappointment rocked me. Why was I always so damned awkward around cute guys? It was probably why it took me so long to finally get rid of Bob, the one hot man who'd paid attention to me. But most of the time his attention had been in not such a nice way with put down insults.

"We're finished, ma'am. Now if you'd please let us show you how it works."

I shook my head. Um, no. The faster they got out of here, the better.

"Oh, no worries. Just leave the instruction manual. I'll be fine," I answered. Wow, was that my voice? It sounded low and husky. Bedroomy. Surely, an ice-cube for each cheek would come in handy about now.

Thomas frowned as he looked down at me.

"Free lessons come with the pleasure machine, ma'am. We cannot leave until we know you understand how everything works. We wouldn't want you to accidentally hurt yourself and end up in the hospital. Besides, we can't leave until you sign the release papers. And you can't sign the release papers until we are assured you know what you are doing. It's mainly for insurance purposes. We don't want to get sued and if we do, and there's no signature then it would be negligence on our side and our insurance company wouldn't cover us. You understand, right?"

Man, this was turning out to be more complicated than I'd thought.

"I had no idea it could be dangerous," I replied. The last thing I wanted was to end up in the hospital and explain why I was there.

"Not if you know how to use it properly," he said with a cute wink.

Point taken.

"Sure, give me a tour of the machine."

Man had I known that I would be subjected to this kind of embarrassment I would never have had such an extravagant present made for myself. If this is how rich people lived with such an intrusion into their privacy, then they could have it.

I followed him down the hall and stopped short as I spied the new occupant of my guest bedroom.

Chapter Two

Wow. The pleasure machine looked great. It was made from wood and shiny stainless steel. If I could get past that it reminded me of a fancy fully-loaded oversized dental chair, then I would admit that it looked awesome.

The arm-chair was full-length, padded and it looked quite comfortable. I could already imagine myself climbing onto it, lying back and letting the machine have its way with me.

At the head area of the machine was what appeared to be a large oak armor with open doors.

"For your privacy, the lounge folds upright and fits right into this armoire. And a key plus backup key keeps your new toy locked up and away from prying eyes," Thomas explained as he held a keychain with two keys dangling from it.

"No one will know you have it," Gerald said with a grin.

I nodded, feeling grateful that my worries about anyone seeing this machine were alleviated. I did a quick visual inspection of my new toy.

There were several metal arms extending from a side section, which was also made of ornately carved oak wood. Attached to the end of each metal extension was a wooden dildo. Each dildo appeared to look life-like in shape with veins intricately interwoven along each shaft. Each piece of carved wood was of a different length and girth, with variously shaped cockheads such as plum-shaped or mushroom-shaped.

Goodness, I was going to have plenty of fun with all these cocks.

"The computer that runs everything is hidden beneath the seat, tucked away so you won't even know it's here," Thomas said.

His voice rocked me back to reality. For a few glorious moments, I'd forgotten these men were here.

I watched Thomas as he bent over and opened an elaborately carved cupboard door beneath the seat of the chaise. Inside, on a black metal console that looked the size of an extra-large desktop computer, blinked several little red lights.

"And on this remote, you'll find everything your heart desires," Gerald said as he grabbed a tv-sized remote from a wood tray that was attached to the machine.

He pressed a button and one of the steel arms moved a dildo and poised it over the chaise.

"When you become an expert at this, you can command a dildo to enter your mouth, another to penetrate your ass and yet another to thrust into your vagina. All at the same time," Gerald said.

Wow, that was incredible.

"Everything is moveable and the dildoes are interchangeable with wooden anal beads, g-spot stimulators, vibrators and even paddles. For now, we've outfitted you with smooth dildoes. When you wish to explore the realm of other adult toys, all made from wood, of course, you'll find everything on our site," Thomas explained. He moved away from the console and waved at the padded chaise.

"The chair lowers until it is flat. You can sit, or lie on it, face up, or face down or sideways. As long as you have the remote nearby, you can program it to do virtually anything."

Gosh, my very own computerized pleasure servant. I truly was stunned at what I had ordered. Truth be told, I had filled out a questionnaire and hadn't really been shown any pictures of what the final product would look like. Their excuse being every customer ordered a different look and the Shoppe didn't share pictures due to privacy issues.

"Okay, let's get down to business," Thomas said as he rubbed his hands together. "We'll need you to fully undress and then you can sit right here on the seat and we can give you a demonstration."

Undress? My mind whirled.

They must have noticed my hesitation.

"We'll need to do some insertions, to show you how everything works," Gerald added.

Insertions? Is he serious?

"The demonstration is included in the price," Gerald continued. The gift certificate you provided comes with many fringe benefits. Didn't the ladies who gave you the present tell you?" Thomas asked.

"No," I answered hurriedly.

Gerald chuckled.

"They probably didn't want to scare you off. Maybe you're just one of the shy ones? Here. I'll take off my shirt, so you won't be alone in your nakedness," Gerald said.

Oh, my Lord.

My throat went dry as he began unbuttoning his plaid shirt, giving me glimpses of a lightly hairy chest and some impressive flexing chest muscles that had me catching my breath.

"I um...I don't think I can undress. This is highly unusual," I muttered.

"You wouldn't want to disappoint your friends, would you?" Thomas asked.

He was gazing at me in what I could only perceive as a challenging look in the way the tips of his lips had upturned ever so gently. Was he daring me with those bright brown eyes? Had he already caught on that I was naïve and stupid in the ways of sex?

I shook my head jerkily. No, I didn't want my besties to have wasted so much money on me.

"We wouldn't want to take the machine all apart and bring it back to the shop with us. Like I said, we can't have you sign the release papers until you know how to use the machine," Gerald prodded.

The last thing I want is to lose my machine. Okay, sure, yeah, them showing me how it works makes sense. Man, I have to stop being such a prude! I need to lighten up and get with the program. They're only here because I ordered a pleasure machine!

My legs trembled as I kicked off my slippers. My hands shook as I began to unbutton my blouse and I watched Gerald as he slid off his pants.

Oh boy. Oh boy. How did I get into this mess?

I had to admit that Gerald had really nice bulging biceps as he pulled off his pants. And such powerful thigh muscles too. Not to mention an enormous package pressing against his underwear. Talk about eye candy.

I blew out a slow breath, shrugged off my blouse and placed it on the dresser.

The two men were watching me as I slipped my fingers beneath the waistband of my track pants. I could hear their breaths, fast and heavy. Could hear my breaths too.

My heart beat with frantic speed against my chest as I lowered my pants over my hips and down my legs and then off. I placed the pants on top of my blouse.

When I turned around, the two men were now busying themselves around the pleasure machine.

I chastised myself. They are not interested in me. I'm just a customer to them. It's not like they're going to force me into anything I don't want. Although the thought of having a forced ménage with the two of them did seem intriguing.

Give your head a shake woman! This is all business.

I needed to get naked fast because the sooner I learned how to use this machine with all the naughty attachments, the faster they were out of here and the quicker I was getting pleasured by my sparkling new toy!

And she was a beauty. It didn't quite look like a dentist chair anymore. I was afraid of dentists, but I wasn't afraid of pleasure. And with all these octopus-like steel tentacles with attachments, I was going to have tons of hot fun.

Taking advantage of their backs toward me, I took a deep breath and removed my bra and slipped out of my panties. Then I just stood there, watching them as they fiddled with the buttons on the remote. For a moment, I was able to forget I was completely naked. That is until they turned their attention to me.

Their eyes widened as they studied me and I swear I detected appreciation in their suddenly hot gazes. Heat fused my entire body. I had to be nuts standing nude in front of two strangers, but I really wanted my machine and it appeared this was the only way I was going to get it.

"Your throne awaits, my princess," Gerald said as he gestured to the seat with a wave of his arm. One padded armrest was raised and I noticed the seat had a three-inch round gap right in the middle.

"You'll need to place your pussy right there on the opening," Thomas instructed.

I nodded jerkily as I inadvertently placed my palm on the padded seat.

"Hey, the seat is warm," I commented.

"Yes, it's heated. Warmth helps to increase your pleasure experience as it simulates another body."

"Oh, I see," I muttered.

Suddenly I was overwhelmed with everything and I could barely walk on my trembling legs as I moved to the machine. I gazed into that hole in the seat and caught my breath when I spied the top part of a life-like wooden plum-shaped cockhead with an attached clit stimulator, I knew exactly what was awaiting my rapidly wet pussy.

"Remember to angle your vagina right over the hole or as close to it as you can get," Thomas said as he held my elbow like a gentleman and helped me onto the seat.

"The dildo will slide right up into you when you push the button on the remote."

Gerald handed me the remote that was filled with buttons and little joysticks.

"Look over there," he said. Reluctantly I pulled my gaze from the remote to see him nod toward something that was leaned up against the far wall. It looked like an identical seat as to the one attached to this chair.

"That one has two openings for double penetration. The instructions are all in the book. We can show you later how easily the seat can be exchanged." He gestured to a thick manual set upon the tray.

"Now let's just get you nicely situated, so you can try out this remote and your machine," Thomas said.

I wiggled my behind to a spot that I believed might be the right area and to my shock Thomas reached down between my thighs. For an instant, I froze as the back of his hand brushed against my labia. His flesh was hot and my pussy clenched at his touch.

"What are you doing?" I breathed.

"Sit with your back right against the chair. You're too far from the hole," he instructed.

That's when I realized he was just exploring to check if I was in the right position. Then he removed his hand and gazed at the remote clutched between my fingers. He leaned closer to me.

His scent of pine mesmerized me and I loved that serious expression on his face as he concentrated on the remote.

"Okay, now let's see. Check the speed here. Speed is on slow. All you do is press this little button with the up arrow and..."

He pressed a blue button and almost instantly something warm nudged against my vaginal opening.

I yelped in surprise.

Thomas and Gerald chuckled.

"You'll feel the heat in the dildo also. You can also ask it to be as cold as ice or other scenarios like mild and cool. Whatever your wish. This is the temperature dial." He pointed to a dial with numbers.

"But let's stick with warm as it simulates a real cock. There's also a speed dial and it's on ultra-slow," Gerald said. I noticed his voice was softer now as he leaned in to point out the dial.

I held my breath and clutched the armrests as the warm, thick dildo stretched past my tight muscles and slid slowly up into my vagina, going ultra-deep before it stopped. I inhaled as my pussy involuntarily clenched around the wide girth.

"Okay, let's keep it nice and snug inside of you for a bit while we check out the other features," Thomas said. His voice had deepened and thickened.

"Oh, and here, you'll want to use these too," Thomas said. I watched as he pressed another button and one of the steel arms came toward me. Something dangled off the end.

"Nipple clamps," Thomas explained.

"May we place them on?" Gerald asked.

My breath hitched. Oh, this was so not what I expected to happen tonight.

I nodded numbly.

To my surprise, both men reached out and before I knew what was happening, each man had cupped a breast and was eagerly plumping my nipples. Pleasure pain had me gasping and I squirmed which made the dildo move inside me. Unexpected arousal shifted through me and I forced myself to sit still.

Gosh! The last thing I wanted was to be aroused in front of two strangers.

But how could I not respond? Their fingers tweaked and pinched until my nipples looked so juicy red and were so tender and pleasure-filled that I couldn't stop myself from gyrating my hips.

"Easy, Colleen. We haven't even started yet," Thomas said with a chuckle.

I inhaled at the sweet painful pressure as each man continued to twist my tenderized flesh.

"For the best performance, you'll also need these restraints to keep you anchored." Gerald's voice sounded strangled and aroused.

Restraints? Huh?

Before I could comprehend his meaning, straps were placed over my wrists and ankles. I tried to move my hands and feet, but the bindings wouldn't budge. A tinge of panic zipped through me.

"You'll need the bindings so you won't fall out of the chair as we bring you way back into a reclining position," Gerald said with a wink.

Okay. That didn't make sense because there were armrests and a footrest to prevent that from happening.

"You have really nice breasts," Gerald whispered in my ear. He'd cupped my breast again and was holding me so intimately like it was some kind of jewel, and I liked the look of appreciation in his blue eyes.

"A sweet body too. It's a shame you'll be hiding in here and letting a machine make love to you instead of men," Thomas muttered.

By now I'd closed my eyes, mesmerized by the seductive tone of their voices. I hadn't even realized doing it, but my senses were becoming quickly overwhelmed as the two strangers snapped the clamps onto my tenderized nipples.

"Oh," I gasped as my taut flesh began to tingle. The clamps squeezed and then loosened and squeezed some more, just like the men's fingers had done.

"It's all in the remote. And as long as you have it within reach, you're in control," Thomas' voice sounded hoarse and something dark underlined his words.

As long as I have that remote in reach...where was the remote?

It wasn't in my hand anymore. I hadn't even felt it being removed.

I opened my eyes and blinked. Who had the remote control?

Chapter Three

Gerald held up the remote and wiggled his eyebrows.

"Got you right where we want you for this demo. Now lie back and enjoy" Gerald said with a smile.

The chair began to recline. The warm dildo inside my vagina shifted into a more pleasurable position and the clit stimulator nudged perfectly against my clitoris.

Oh yes! This is nice.

"There's just one thing that this machine doesn't simulate," Thomas said.

"Huh? What's that?" As far as I was concerned this pleasure machine would go above and beyond the call of duty.

There was a sensual tone in his voice that had me opening my eyes. Gosh, I hadn't even realized I'd closed them again.

Thomas was close to me now. So close that I noticed his brown hair was the exact same color of his eyes. His eyes were so dark that they were almost black. I could even see gold flecks in the chocolate-colored layers of his iris'. Gold and brown was an exquisite color combination. It reminded me of the edible 24 karat gold flakes that were sprinkled on the delicious Tuscany-made dark chocolate pudding that my girlfriends bought me when I went out with them to one of the fancy New York restaurants they frequented.

"Your new machine can do plenty of pleasuring, but a machine can't do this," Thomas said.

He leaned forward and brushed his lips against my neck. Erotic tingles seared through me and awareness buzzed in my heaving breasts, my lower belly and between my thighs.

Wow, why was I reacting like this to him? I should be screaming bloody murder, shouldn't I? Having been tied down by them and with this behavior being...so inappropriate.

Then Thomas' hot mouth fused over mine and my nerve endings throughout my body zinged to life.

All thoughts of protest shattered.

His lips sucked and nibbled creating a killing pleasure that had me trembling and moaning as sensations rocked me. His mouth devoured me and I whimpered as he thrust his tongue between my lips. Shyly, I opened and his velvety tongue slipped past my teeth and sensually stroked my tongue.

I gasped as the dildo moved out and then back into me again, the clitoris stimulator rubbing sensuously against my clit. In and out. Erotically massaging. Shivery sensations. Clamps sensually squeezing my nipples. Fever heat. Whew! I'd never felt so hot.

Fingers stroked my bare breasts. Hands, large and work-roughened, carnally explored my curves, my hips, my belly and along my inner thighs. My breaths were coming faster and faster, my body tightening and tensing so hard that I knew I was going to explode at any second.

Suddenly I didn't care that this shouldn't be happening. Didn't care that two complete strangers were seducing me. Didn't care that I was about to lose all shred of decency allowing this to happen.

The dildo grew warmer and began to thrust quicker, rougher, deeper. The clamps twisted and pulled. Thomas kissed me harder.

I imagined Thomas thrusting his cock into me. Imagined Gerald's hot mouth sucking on my nipples. Lightning bolts of pleasure forked through me. Sensations snapped deep inside my vagina. My inner thighs quivered.

I shuddered and came apart. I bucked and keened and writhed.

Oh God! This pleasure was insane.

Encouraging whispers echoed in my ears. Come. Come. Come, Gerald chanted.

I trembled and undulated. Struggled against the restraints. Clenched my hands as sensual shudders rocked me. Searing bites of pleasure dragged me under, tossed me up and then swirled me under a blanket of wicked jolts.

Thomas broke the kiss and I frantically sucked in cool air as I convulsed and wept. For a few seconds, my fragmented mind began to reform but before I could have a semblance of a co-ordinated thought the dildo began moving in and out of me at an incredible speed. Tension mounted. Another erotic storm swelled and I quickly rocked into a second orgasm.

This one was stronger than the last.

I wailed and as the dildo thrust so fast it created an impressive friction. My body became so inflamed with shudders. It was insane.

God! This was so good!

I became suspended on a pleasure rack. My pussy throbbed and pulsed. My nipples felt ten times their size. I gasped and sucked in air as I rode the shimmering waves. Pleasure zinged and zipped throughout my flesh and I could literally feel the heat waves coming off my body.

I cried out as a third climax began to wind through me.

Suddenly my restraints were magically gone and I was being lifted from the chair and set upon my feet. I almost collapsed as my legs were like rubber. I could barely see Gerald as he stood in front of me, an erotic grin tilting the sides of his luscious lips.

"We've got protection," Gerald growled as he gazed downward.

I blinked. I hadn't even thought about protection. This was all happening so fast. My head was spinning, but my body was eager.

I followed his gaze and stilled as I saw his erection. His cock was large and thick and my swollen vagina clenched involuntarily at his size, making me catch my breath. He was gripping his condom-sheathed shaft and I could easily see the pulsing blue veins interwoven along the nine-inch length as well as the smooth plum-shaped cockhead.

"You like what you see?" Gerald asked as he continued to stroke himself.

I shuddered and nodded numbly.

"I...I haven't..." How could I tell them I'd never been with two men. Tell them that this shouldn't be happening.

But the words just wouldn't form.

How could I turn down the sexual attention of two well-muscled men?

"You haven't been with two men?" Thomas asked as he suddenly appeared beside Gerald. He was completely naked and my mouth went dry as I saw his shaft. It was huge and looked like an enormous serpent as it curved upward toward his taut belly.

I nodded jerkily.

"A ménage virgin?" Gerald asked. He appeared surprised.

"You aren't like your friends? Worldly in the ways of sex?" Thomas asked.

I felt embarrassed and shrugged my shoulders.

"We'll give you a good time," Thomas murmured.

I tensed as he circled around toward my back and placed his calloused palms upon my waist.

"Are you ready to be taken?" Gerald asked.

Good Lord.

What was going to happen to me? Couldn't I take two large cocks into me?

They didn't wait for an answer and suddenly I was being sandwiched between two heated male bodies. My breathing escalated as I instinctively knew I was going to be in for a rough ride.

Thomas' hot lips sucked my left earlobe into his mouth. Swirling sensations promised pleasure as tingles rippled up and down my spine.

"Look at me, Collen. Let me see your pretty green eyes as I penetrate you," Gerald crooned.

My eyelids were so heavy so I could barely keep them open. Could barely see, but I noticed Gerald's expression was tight with arousal and he was hungry for sex. His shoulders were broad, and muscles rippled across his chest as he reached out and splayed his hands over my hips.

I inhaled as his engorged shaft pressed against my opening.

"You first," Gerald whispered.

I wasn't sure what he was talking about until a wide flared cockhead pushed into my ass. I cried out at the burning pressure of my anal muscles expanding and then clutching his rigid flesh.

I whimpered as Gerald's firm lips took possession of my mouth. He kissed harder than Thomas. Hard and dominating.

I fought to breathe as the wet heat of his lips teased and coerced me to open my mouth to him. Then he drove his thick tongue in and made love to my tongue with sensual swirls that left me heady.

Pleasure-pain snapped through me as Thomas fiercely thrust into my ass and I moaned as pleasure-pain awakened highly sensitive nerve endings.

"There, there," Thomas whispered and raked his teeth along the side of my neck, leaving behind a fiery heat.

Thomas withdrew, and I arched against both men as Gerald drove into me with a frenzied lunge. He withdrew quickly and then Thomas impaled me again. The bulging length of his thick shaft pulsed deep inside and my muscles involuntarily clenched tight around the erotic invasion.

Thomas groaned and pulled out.

Both men held tight to me as they quickly dropped into a sensual rhythm, their combined thrusts driving me toward exquisite tension. I fought to accept the invasion of the two of them. They overstretched me and the sharp bites of erotic pain had me keening.

They bucked against me and thrust into me until perspiration swept over my heated body and a heady anticipation rolled through me.

The rapturous tremors came out of nowhere, raging and growing until I was tumbling within an explosive force. Carnal waves shattered over me and I was sinking into red-hot bliss and drowning in erotic fury. I cried out and gyrated as ecstasy held me captive.

Gerald melded his mouth over mine again, catching my keens and cries.

Both men rocked harder. Their long shafts reaching depths and unleashing dark desires I never knew I possessed.

Their hips banged against me as their shafts drove deeper and deeper. Strong-hard erections jerked and throbbed and pistoned. Their bodies were like molten steel keeping me hostage. I moaned and strained between them as uncontrollable shudders pummelled me. Pleasure surged, and I exploded into yet another orgasm.

My breaths sawed through me like wild-fire. My pussy clenched and I was drenched with cream. My nipples were hyper-sensitive, as hard-packed male muscles brushed and rasped against them.

The sucking sounds of their cocks leaving my quivering holes rippled through the air and their grunts and groans were like mesmerizing music in my ears.

Vaguely I was able to form a thought. Who needed a pleasure machine when I had these two hot carpenters doing such a great job in pleasuring me?

Oh wow! I never wanted to come out of this pleasure vortex! This was so good. Too good to be true.

An insistent buzzing sound rattled through my climax and I came awake on a moan. Beneath the sheets, my hand was sawing between my thighs, my fingers rubbing my extra-sensitized clit as I undulated my hips frantic for another release. My body was tense, and I was so aroused I knew I was about to come.

I blinked as sunshine streamed through my apartment window.

What? What was going on? Where were Thomas and Gerald?

I blinked some more.

A dream? Had this all been a sex dream?

No. No. No.

God, they'd made me feel so good. I wanted more of this exquisite pleasure. I wanted more.

Disappointment rocked me. How could I go on living without such racy pleasure? I blew out a tense breath and moaned at my pouty pussy and clenching ass. I needed penetration. I needed Thomas and Gerald.

The buzzing sound that had awoken me screamed into my confusion. My apartment buzzer? Someone was in the lobby trying to contact me. Who?

Damn, I'd drank too much alcohol last night. Alcohol did that to me. It screwed with my memory the morning after.

I'd stayed up so late last night after having been caught in a writer's high while working on a current story. Many glasses of cheap white wine and several hours had passed before I'd realized I had to grab some sleep. I'd barely been able to drag my tipsy self into bed in the wee hours of the morning and I'd slept so deeply that I must have dreamed about all that hot and heavy sex with the two carpenters.

Man, my entire body was on fire. I was primed. I needed to masturbate myself right out of this sexual awareness.

I rubbed my clit and moaned at the incredible pleasure melting over me.

The buzzer rang again.

Shit. Go away!

Another buzz. This time the irritating sound went on even longer. Whoever was down in the lobby was not going to go away.

I moaned my frustration and pushed aside my comforter. Chilly air embraced me and I knew instantly the faulty thermostat was acting up again.

The cobwebs of sleep made it hard for me to focus on who the hell was here as I stumbled out of bed and wandered naked down the hallway.

The buzzer rang again.

Insistent, weren't they?

"Hello?" I answered.

I heard no reply and I realized I hadn't even pressed the intercom button.

Man! I was really out of it this morning.

"Yeah, hello?" I said after pushing the button.

"The Sexy Wooden Toy Shoppe here, ma'am. Thomas and Gerald. We have an appointment with Colleen. May we come to set up your order?"

My heart went into overdrive. Heat fused through me and I brightened.

Oh yeah, now I remembered. They'd emailed a few days ago to let me know the sex machine was ready. They were going to set up the pleasure machine and demonstrate how it would work. But that was on Saturday morning. Was it already Saturday?

Suddenly the sex dream I'd just had came rolling into full focus. Anticipation and arousal screamed through me and for some inexplicable reason I knew why my friend, Grace, had winked at me during my "first-month anniversary breakup with Bob party" when she'd said the carpenters would show me how everything works.

Without a doubt, I knew I could go through with those fringe benefits, especially in the sultry way I was feeling.

To hell with vanilla sex. I was ready to explore everything.

"Yes, please. Do come," I answered and grinned.

There was no way those two men were leaving my apartment today without making my sex dreams come true and I meant that quite literally.

The End

Jasmine Black Mini Catalog

Pleasured By Her Guards
A Three Book Collection
Jasmine Black
These naughty guards truly misbehave...

~

Taken by Two Prison Guards
Jasmine Black
Twenty-three-year-old Madeline "Mad" Madison has quite the temper. She got ten years to life in prison due to her getting mad at her late boyfriend and there's only one way she knows of to keep herself calm and she's not getting *that* type of rehabilitation in prison. That is, until she's assigned hard labor and taken by two naughty prison guards.

*

Taken by Two Lifeguards
Jasmine Black

Twenty-two-year-old professional swimmer and Olympic hopeful, Katie White, goes to the beach every day to continue work on her training by swimming in the ocean...and to do some secret naughty stuff on the side.

She also loves the lifeguard eye candy. Skimpy swim trunks on tanned muscular bodies put her in a really good mood. But the lifeguards don't seem to know she exists, especially after she broke up with her lifeguard boyfriend, Chad.

When Katie suddenly gets caught in a malicious storm, two lifeguards come to her rescue. One of them is Chad!

Stranded in the first-aid shack and being almost dead has made Katie awfully cold and her two lifeguard rescuers are going to warm Katie up nice and slow...

*

Taken by Three Bodyguards
Jasmine Black

Twenty-one-year-old Stephanie Stephenson has been in a safehouse with her three sexy bodyguards for many months. She's a lone witness to a murder and they've been protecting her from Santonio, the mob boss, who has vowed revenge if she dared to testify. It's all been strictly professional and platonic with her hunky bodyguards. Now the trial is over and Stephanie is free to go.

But her three bodyguards have other plans for Stephanie...very naughty plans.

Other stories by Jasmine

Taken by Three Doctors, Taken by Three Bikers, Taken by Three Billionaires, Taken by Two Cowboys, Taken by Three Cowboys, Taken by Two Santas, Taken by Two Elves, Taken by Three Bodyguards, Taken by Two Cops, Taken by Two Prison Guards, Taken by Two Lifeguards, Taken by Two Mountain Men, Taken by Two Sugar Daddies and more!

About the Author

Jasmine Black lives in Ontario, Canada.

By day she writes erotic romances under another pseudonym and by night she writes erotica ménage.

She enjoys hiking, photography, gardening, exploring, reading and writing.

You can find more about Jasmine and her stories at http://www.jasmine-black.com